SEARCH FOR THE MEDALLION

(Gateskin Chronicles, Book 3)

JANICE SPINA

PUBLISHED BY JANICE SPINA

Londonderry, New Hampshire

COVER BY JOHN SPINA

ISBN (paperback) 979-8-9874646-4-9

Library of Congress Control Number: 2024908390

ACKNOWLEDGEMENTS

A very special thank you to my wonderful beta readers, Patricia Bradley, Michelle Clement James, Michele Rolfe, John Spina, and Frances Stewart for working tirelessly to read and review my work and for their helpful input. Their assistance is invaluable and appreciated.

Thank you to my husband, John, for the beautiful cover and for all the dinners he cooked that made it possible for me to write.

DEDICATION

This fantasy is dedicated to my husband, John, who has been patient enough to read this book about magic and fantasy in which he does not always believe. I think at the conclusion of this book he may now be a believer of fantasy and magic.

For all your support and encouragement, John, I thank you and love you dearly.

To all who believe in magic and fantasy

Table of Contents

MAP OF TERRITORY OF NOELLA PROVINCE

CHARACTERS

Serena (14) - heroine of story, sister to Simon and Catalina

Simon (12) - brother of Serena and Catalina

Catalina (10) - sister of Serena and Simon

Solinara - Queen Fairy of Sovorotskina and mother of Serena and siblings

Gateskin - King Wizard of Sovorotskina and father of Serena and Siblings

Sovorotskina - Land of Goodness and Light, home of Serena and Family

Ressaphena - Goddess of Goodness and Light

Ramoforan- God of Goodness and Light

Noella - surviving child of Sovorotskina, during the capture of Taken Ones became Queen Fairy of Votovia

Sonovan - 1st King Wizard,
husband of Noella,
and ruler of Votovia

Noella II - descendant of Noella only child survivor of Legend of Taken Ones

Josoforan - King of Sovorotskina during capture of Taken Ones

Marolena - Queen Fairy of Sovorotskina during capture of Taken Ones

Hotenfaran - Wizard, uncle of Serena and siblings, brother of Queen Solinara

Procelina - Fairy, aunt of Serena and siblings

Arubane – adopted son of Procelina and Hotenfaran with many powers

Toleran - citizen guard of Sovorotskina

Miserva - citizen of Sovorotskina and wife of Toleran

Peteran - young son of Toleran & Miserva of Sovorotskina

Amora - Land of Faith and Love

Noderan - elder Amorans subject (Became King of Amora)

Davora – wife of Noderan
(Became Queen of Amora)

Merlina - Land of Magic and Mystery

Merlinans - citizens of Merlina

Merona - Land of Myths and Legends

(Named after Fairy Princess captured by EO)

Meronans - citizens of Merona

Votovia - Land of Peace and Harmony

Votovians - peaceful but powerful subjects of Votovia

Savina - Queen Fairy of Votovia, present day ruler

Cavelan - King Wizard of Votovia, present day ruler

Adolphin - son of king and queen of Votovia

Anatonia Noella - daughter of king and queen of Votovia

Soneran - member of King Cavelan's guard

Latoran - member of King Cavelan's guard

Sprites - little tree people who lived in the forests around Sovorotskina and the other villages

Spindle - tree Sprite, friend of Serena's

Abason - tree Sprite, father of Spindle, Head Counsel of Sprites

Anabal - tree Sprite, mother of Spindle

Micah - brother of Abason, captured by Evil Ones

Parotovina - Land of Darkness and Evil, home of Evil Ones

Beregina - Queen Witch of Parotovina

Kaposkaran - King Wizard of Parotovina

Parotovinans - citizens of Parotovina

Quilarena - Goddess of Darkness and Evil

Quilottan - God of Darkness and Evil

Mitteran - Head Guard of scouting party of Parotovinans

Leanna - wife of Mitteran

Allonso (Al) - son of Mitteran & Leanna

Tessa- daughter of Mitteran & Leanna

Kelleran – Gatekeeper of Parotovina

Francia – wife of Kelleran

Botular – Eyes & ears of King Kaposkaran (HOH – becomes citizen of Sovorotskina)

Zuri - King of Merlina

Zuleima - Queen of Merlina

Zayleen - daughter of King Zuri/Queen Zuleima

Zukan - son of King Zuri/Queen Zuleima

Zuriann - daughter of King Zuri/Queen Zuleima

Cantok – large wolf from Unknown Territory – migrated to Sovorotskina

Notak – mate of Cantok

Tankor – male cub of Cantok

Rattor – male cub of Cantok

Maku – female cub of Cantok

Rabbinels – creatures created by Queen Solinara and Hotenfaran to feed the wolves and fulfill the need of the wolves to hunt and forage for food

Quintaroon – a creature created by the Wizards of Parotovina

Catlings – cat-like creatures that roam the UT

Animals in King Gateskin Barn - chickens, Milly the cow, Hank the horse, goats

Acronyms:

EVIL ONES - EOs

TAKEN ONES - TOs

DESCENDANTS OF TOs - Ds

UNKNOWN TERRITORY - UT

Parotovinan Wizards - Head Wizard - Marno

Wizard #2 - Fortag

Wizard #3 - Wassor

Wizard #4 - Tornak

Wizard #5 - Kerno

Wizard #6 - Sufan

Parotovinans with powers

Henno & Jenara - husband & wife

Danko - kind Parotovinan guard

Garita - wife of Danko

Harmony - daughter of Danko & Garita

Celdrick - son of Danko & Garita

Aneka - daughter of Danko & Garita

Dargonet - God of Dark Magic

Aharona - sister of Navaeha from Dragonaria

Callum - Aharona's dragon

Nevaeha - Aharona's sister

Evander - Navaeha's dragon

Isla and Marcellus - parents of Aharona and Nevaeha and rulers of island of Dragonaria - Land of Dragons

Elowen - evil sister of Aharona and Nevaeha

Jelitza - cousin of Aharona and Navaeha

Verite - female dragon belonging to Jelitza

Mianna - friend of Elowen

VILLAGES:

Sovorotskina - Land of Goodness & Light - King Gateskin/Queen Solinara

Parotovina - Land of Evil & Darkness King Kaposkaran/Queen Beregina

Votovia - Land of Magic & Mystery - King Cavelan/Queen Savina

Amora - Land of Faith & Love - King Noderan/Queen Davora

Merona - Land of Peace & Harmony - Ruled by Healers

Merlina - Land of Myths & Legends - King Zuri/Queen Zuleima

Dragonaria - Land of Dragons - island south of Novella Province - King Marcellinus/Queen Isla

CHAPTER ONE

There was green moss covering the land in some of the villages. It appeared to be moving in a slow, melodious way as if an invisible hand was guiding it along.

King Gateskin couldn't believe his eyes. He had to do something before it reached his own village of Sovorotskina.

He opened the Channel Spell to conference with the other rulers of the neighboring villages. He had to warn them, if they did not already know, what was happening.

When the conference began, all the rulers cried out in alarm, "We know! We saw this moss moving and growing, Gateskin. But we can't seem to stop it! It is moving like a snake and covering everything in its way," Ruler of Merlina, King Zuri, exclaimed, in a tremulous voice, as he watched helplessly from the high tower in his castle.

The other rulers agreed. The Healers of Merona suggested, "Maybe we can ask King Kaposkaran of Parotovina to have his wife, Queen Beregina, turn off the spell she created to capture the Catlings." These are large cat-like creatures who live in the UT, Unknown Territory.

"No, I don't think that would be a good idea," King Gateskin responded as he continued to ponder what would be the best avenue to pursue.

King Cavelan of Votovia spoke up, disturbing the silence that hung over the group, "I think it is the Dark God, the one whose name we should not mention. He may be still here and trying to take over our lands."

King Gateskin held his hands up to calm everyone as he said, "It may be, but I don't think so. At least, I hope it isn't him."

King Noderan of Amora, asked, "What do you think it is, Gateskin?"

King Gateskin hung his head and covered his eyes with his hands as he concentrated. "I think it is the residual effects of the spell created by Queen Beregina of Parotovina that we must turn back before it covers all the lands."

"Do you think it will be irreversible if it does cover everything?" The Healers enquired as they exchanged worried glances.

"That, I don't know, Healers. But I plan to find out quickly with all your help. If we combine our powers, we can begin to curb the spread of this substance that appears to be some kind of moss-like substance. Stay away from it in case it still can put anyone to sleep like it did to the Catlings."

"I think it still has that power, Gateskin. One of my sheep fell over after it ate some of it," Zuri exclaimed in alarm.

"Tell all your men to stay away from it and warn your citizens to stay inside until we can deal with this," Gateskin announced in a strong voice.

"Should we keep this Channel Spell open as we deal with this situation,

Gateskin?" King Cavelan, ruler of Votovia, asked, anxiously.

"Yes, that is a good idea, Cavelan. That way we can see where it is at all times. Have your Wizards work on spells to curb it any way they can. I will do the same."

CHAPTER TWO

Animals throughout the kingdoms were falling asleep after ingesting the moss. Citizens scurried around trying to keep their animals from succumbing to this substance. They locked the animals inside their barns or stables after making sure no moss was inside.

The people of the surrounding villages tried everything to revive the animals who were asleep. They threw cold water on them and shook them. Some animals awakened, startled, and confused, while others slept on. It appeared these slumbering animals were ones who had ingested more of the moss than the others.

King Gateskin kept speaking to his people and informing them what to do next if the moss spread to Sovorotskina. This strange moss was creeping along at a faster pace now and was going to be entering Sovorotskina soon if not stopped.

The King's Wizards stood at the borders of Sovorotskina and spread their spells over the kingdom. The moss stopped as the latest spell touched it. It began to shrink away slowly and dry up. The Wizards kept spreading the spell which now was known as the Moss Spell all around the boundaries and shared it with the other village Wizards.

Soon the moss was shriveling up and dying all over Noella Province except in Parotovina, Land of Darkness and Evil. When it reached this stage, King Gateskin and the other rulers commanded their guards to begin pulling up the moss and burning it in barrels away from the population. This was the only way to rid the province of its detrimental properties once and for all. The men soon noticed they felt sleepy if they breathed in the smoke and had to cover their mouths and noses until the burning was complete and the smoke diminished.

***

The only ruler who did not take part in this process was King Kaposkaran. He refused to listen to anyone and said he would rid the moss on his own.

King Kaposkaran had his men drop off the sleeping Catlings back into the UT where they belonged after the creatures had ingested the moss created by the spell of Kaposkaran's wife, Queen Beregina. These creatures had wreaked havoc in their land and there was no other way to get rid of them. The spell, however, came dangerously close to Dark Magic when the Queen could not stop it.

Deep in the Unknown Territory, Catlings, and other smaller creatures now awakened, after ingesting the moss, hungry and prowling around for food.

These Catlings quickly captured the smaller animals who were still groggy and not able to move as fast as they normally could to escape.

Soon the Catlings would have no food if they kept eating this voraciously. This would cause trouble once again for the lands if the Catlings ventured out of the UT to search for sustenance.

CHAPTER THREE

If anyone had looked up into the sky, they would have seen there were two large objects flying toward the UT. The Catlings were unaware of these objects; they were too busy eating their way through the forest.

The large objects coming that way were two dragons ridden by their mistresses, sisters, Aharona and Nevaeha, from another land far away. Aharona sat upon the back of Callum, a multi-colored dragon with scales that were iridescent and sparkled in the sunlight as it flew along making it appear that there was a rainbow in the sky. Callum was a sweet dragon but still fierce when he needed to be to protect his mistress.

Navaeha, the younger of the sisters, rode Evander, a brilliant blue, red and gold dragon, with larger wings and a fierce expression, evidence of his internal personality that was anything but friendly to anyone who came close to him except Navaeha, who he adored and obeyed. May the gods protect anyone else who ventured too close or ever thought to threaten Navaeha.

The sisters had been traveling for hours and had stopped just to eat and sleep along the way on islands that they had passed. Their home was far from here on the island of Dragonaria, Land of Dragons. This land is inhabited by people who train the dragons in order to live with them in peace and safety. Not all the islanders are skilled at training these creatures. These people fear the dragons and keep their distance from them.

Aharona and Navaeha are skilled dragon tamers and trainers. They have been doing this since they were old enough to walk and talk. They were taught by their parents, Queen Isla, their mother, and King Marcellus, their father, who are the rulers of the island. The girls also have an older sister named Elowen. She does not get along with them and lives on the other side of the island away from the dragons. Elowen is known to practice Dark Magic which is not allowed, but somehow, she gets away with it by doing it in her hideaway.

The two younger sisters avoid any contact with Elowen since they do not see eye to eye on anything. They do not like what she does or how she behaves toward their parents or to them. Elowen was pure evil. They hated to even think that, but it was true.

They also had a younger cousin named Jelitza who was just sixteen. She had her own dragon, Verite, whose scales were silver. She had a sweet personality but was determined to be the best female dragon on Dragonaria. Verite often had to compete with the males for food and sport. She never backed down. Her mistress Jelitza was fearless herself. Together they could be quite a formidable pair. Jelitza often visited with Aharona and Navaeha and tended to shadow them.

The sisters knew Jelitza might try to follow them so they told her they had a job to do for their father and would return soon. They knew Jelitza did not like to work too hard.

Each day the sisters ventured further away from Dragonaria. They were bored with their everyday chores and life and so were their dragons who also sought adventure.

The sisters decided one day to try to find this land far to the north they had heard about. This land was supposed to be divided into different lands or villages, all part of the large province of Noella. Each village supposedly had its own ruler. They had never heard of such a thing for one land to be divided in this way. Their island was one even though it did have its separate villages and peoples; they were all ruled by one leader, their father.

They had also heard that a Wizard had buried a Medallion somewhere on this land but others who had searched, had never found it. They wanted to do their own search to see if they could recover it.

Hovering over the forested land below them, the sisters began their descent to discover if this was the land they sought.

CHAPTER FOUR

The Catlings heard a sound coming from above and stopped eating to look up. What they saw made them run for their lives.

Aharona called out to her sister, "Look over there. What kind of animals are they?"

"I don't know. I've never seen anything like that. I wonder if they like human or dragon meat. They are quite large and look like overgrown cats," Nevaeha stated in awe.

"Well, I guess they don't like dragons. Thank goodness. I don't think they will be back too soon. They even left their dinner here."

"Maybe Callum and Evander can now have a snack," Nevaeha giggled.

The sisters settled down and let the dragons go over and check out the unfinished meat. They looked around and noted the trees were quite thick and made the area look dark as if a cloak was covering the land.

"Where are we, Aharona?"

"I don't know. There aren't any buildings around or people. The whole area appears to be deserted and untouched by humans. These creatures have possibly killed off all life to survive."

"You could be right, Nevaeha. That means we must be watchful and not let our guard down. Those creatures are probably observing us as we speak, just waiting for a chance to grab us for their dinner."

"I'm not worried at all with Evander and Callum close by. They would never let anyone or anything harm us."

"I hope you are right, sister. But I am still going on the alert. We should move away from here. Let's hop on our rides and find another place more suitable that doesn't have these creatures."

"You don't have to say that twice, Aharona. I am ready when you are.

Let's see if Evander and Callum have had their fill. It's not good to interrupt a hungry dragon from eating."

"I don't think you have to worry about that, Nevaeha. Evander loves you so much that he would excuse anything you did. Don't you remember the first time you found him? You couldn't have been more than three years old."

"Ah, yes! That was quite a discovery for me at a young age, to see a dragon like him up close. Father didn't know you had taken me for a walk that day. He thought we were only going to stay close to our village. But of course, I was the one to wander a little further out where the dragons were nesting."

"You always were a daredevil, Nevaeha. I couldn't stop you in time before you had gone right up to the sleeping dragon and poked him on his nose."

"That was so funny, Aharona! I laughed right after I did it until the dragon opened his huge blue eyes and looked right at me, almost nose to nose. I began to hiccup like I do when I am nervous. He didn't know what to do with me. When his eyes grew larger, I hiccupped more and then fell over laughing at the look on his face."

"You can laugh now but I was terrified he would eat you. You were so small and could have fit into his large jaw and been a tasty treat. Father and mother would have killed me!" Aharona stated, with a heavy sigh.

"I don't know if they would have gone that far, Aharona," Navaeha giggled at her sister's response. "I told you not to tell them, but it didn't matter since Evander followed us home. Remember Father's shock when he saw us leading the dragon into the village?"

"Yes, I thought he was going to have a heart attack and mother nearly passed out. I was out of my mind too." Aharona wiped her brow in exasperation.

"I know. It was too funny especially since Evander didn't know what was going on. He did not have a name at the time and had no idea what was happening. He wore the funniest expression on his face, I couldn't help but laugh. I had to give him a name right away since he had adopted me and wouldn't leave my side," Navaeha said with a look of adoration at her beloved dragon.

"He definitely was as smitten with you as you were with him," her sister responded with a giggle.

"Father wasn't at all happy with either of us, Aharona. But he didn't dare get too close to me since Evander was there and looking back at him with a fierce expression that father did not want to test."

"Yes, it was comical to see our father, who is not afraid of anything, be intimidated by this dragon." Both sisters guffawed more as they reminisced.

"That feels like so long ago, Sister," Aharona sighed. "Now you are all grownup and the mistress of a formidable dragon. I may not have told you but I am extremely proud of you."

"You don't have to say that, Aharona. It's not necessary. I know you love me and are proud of me. I love you and am proud of you too."

"Okay. Enough of this, Navaeha. Let's take a look below. This land is greener than any I have ever seen before. This must be the place we were seeking. The Wizard did say the Medallion was buried in a land of green as far as the eye could see."

"Look closely, Aharona. The green appears to be moving. Do you see that? Now it suddenly stopped moving and is turning brown. I wonder what that is?"

"Let's go down and take a closer look. Be careful in case there are more of those cat-like creatures and who knows what else. We don't want to frighten any inhabitants there either. They may never have seen dragons before."

"Yes, I am looking. I don't see anyone in this area. Let's find a place to land." Turning to Evander, Navaeha whispered in his ear, "Find a place to land away from anyone or anything."

Evander nodded for he understood her words and began his dive down to a deserted area.

Once settled on the ground the sisters jumped off their respective dragons and looked around. There was no one about but they could hear some water flowing close by and saw plenty of trees that were a distance away from them.

"The trees over there appear to close in the area where the cat-like creatures were. Maybe this is a spell the people put there to keep the creatures away from them," Navaeha surmised.

"I agree, Navaeha. It looks like that to me too. I would not be surprised if that is what these people did to protect themselves from the dangers. Those cats are hungry and may try to get through eventually once they decimate their feeding source there."

"I don't think I want to be around when they do, Aharona. They were ugly creatures with their large jaws, huge eyes, and long claws that could rip your heart out. I've never seen anything like them before. Of course, in our land we don't have anything like that with our dragons around. They would eat them for dinner."

"Do you want to take a walk and see if we can find the villages? I don't see anything nearby," Aharona inquired and waited for her sister to respond.

"Yes, but we must be careful. These people may not be too friendly. We better tell our dragons to behave themselves and not get into any trouble while we are gone," Navaeha responded with a smirk. "You know how they can be when we are not around to watch them. They get a little silly and wrestle and cause all kinds of havoc."

"Um, right. I remember," Aharona said as she turned to Callum and whispered to him to behave and keep an eye on Evander.

Navaeha leaned in close to Evander and did the same but added, "I will have a treat for you if you are especially good and keep an eye on Callum. We can't afford to get these lands upset with us."

Evander nodded and showed his teeth in a dragon-like smile which would have frightened anyone else but Navaeha who just snickered and patted him on the head and kissed his nose which made the dragon sigh happily and settle down for a nap.

Callum settled next to Evander and they both put up their defenses of camouflage by blending into their surroundings so no one would see them.

Aharona and Navaeha looked back and noticed this when they couldn't see their dragons. "Wow, they still shock me when they do that!" Aharona exclaimed and smiled in relief that now they wouldn't have to worry about anyone stumbling onto their dragons.

What the sisters didn't realize was someone had already seen them.

CHAPTER FIVE

Queen Fairy Solinara of Sovorotskina looked out the window and called her children, “Serena, Simon, Catalina, time for lunch.”

The three children were powerful fairies and a Wizard in their own rights like their father, King Wizard Gateskin and their mother Queen Fairy Solinara. Their parents worried even more as the children's powers increased and threatened to be more powerful than their own.

When the children did not appear, Solinara called out to her husband who had just closed the window to his conference with the rulers of the other villages. "Gateskin, have you seen the children?"

Gateskin came into the kitchen and rubbed his hands together as he responded, "No, dear. I haven't seen them all morning but of course, I've been tied up in my conference room. I'm starving, Solinara. What did you conjure up today?"

"For your information, I did not conjure up anything. I made these sandwiches with the leftovers from yesterday's ham."

"Oh, sorry dear. I didn't mean to insult you that way. I know you are a magician with food even when not using your powers."

"That's better, my love. Here, I made you two sandwiches with extra pickles from my pickling last year. They should add a little spice and saltiness to your mouth."

"Hmm, I can't wait. My mouth is salivating now more than ever."

"Where are the children, dear? I may have to go out there to find them. I hope they did not venture too far and get into some trouble."

"Why don't you call Spindle? He may know where they are. He is usually close to them to save the day whenever they are in trouble."

"Ha, you may be right, dear. I will do that."

Solinara stepped outside and called up to the trees, "Spindle, if you can hear me, please find my children, and tell them to come home for lunch. You are welcome to join them too."

Spindle, a tree Sprite and the King's Head Guard, was sitting up in his tree home looking off into the distance when he heard Queen Fairy Solinara's words.

He called back to her, "I will get them for you, my queen, right away."

Spindle flew over the area and looked around. What he saw was not what he expected. He blinked his eyes a few times and rubbed them to make sure what he saw was real.

He flew closer to take a better look. There was something down there that appeared to be under camouflage. He could see, with his special vision, something large, in fact, two large bodies hiding out there. Coming close to these camouflaged bodies were the three children of Solinara and Gateskin. They did not appear to see these bodies and would bump into them soon if he did not stop them.

He jumped into the nearby tree and whispered down to the children, “Stop where you are. I am coming down there.”

Serena looked up when she heard Spindle’s voice. “What’s going on?” she asked him with a smile.

Serena and Spindle had a special relationship since they were very young. They were smitten with one another and seldom left each other’s side. Spindle had been on their previous adventures and had saved the children countless times from danger, along with his fellow Sprites.

"I don't think you can see what is there but, there are two large bodies a few feet in front of you. I don't know what they are but they could be dangerous. I don't want you harmed, Serena, you or your siblings," he quickly added as he melted from her dazzling smile. She could always warm his heart with just a look from her beautiful green eyes. He sighed happily and shook his head to come to his senses. This was serious. He had to find out what was sitting there in front of them.

"I know what they are, Spindle," Serena whispered. "We were taking a walk to find some mushrooms for my mother's casserole tonight. She asks us to do that sometimes. While we were heading this way, we heard voices. They sounded like women and as we peeked through the trees, we saw two women and their dragons. I couldn't believe how big and beautiful they were!" Serena gushed.

"What, the women?" Spindle joked watching his love's expression as her eyes grew large and spit fire at him.

"No, silly! I was talking about the dragons." Serena punched Spindle in the arm so hard that he fell over. Spindle was only three feet tall which was tall for a Sprite. Most Sprites were a foot tall or less.

Spindle jumped back up and rubbed his sore arm and sighed with a smile. "Was that like a love tap, Serena?"

"No, I…I'm sorry I didn't mean to do that. Did I hurt you, Spindle?" She bent down to look at the Sprite's arm and rub it tenderly as she brushed his hair back from his brown eyes.

"I…I…am okay, Serena. Now tell me about the dragons. What colors were they and did they spit fire?" Spindle asked with wide-eyed wonder.

"No fire, but they were there one minute and then gone the next like magic. They were quite colorful as rainbows and breathtakingly gorgeous."

"Hmm, I see. What about the women you heard talking? Where did they go?"

"They headed toward our village. Maybe we should report this to Father and Mother."

Simon, who was a couple years younger than Serena, perked up and said, "I want to be the one to tell Father."

Catalina, the youngest, two years younger than Simon, had to put in her own opinion as always. "Can't I be the one to tell Father for a change? You two always get to do the fun things."

Simon looked at Serena and nodded, "Okay, Catalina. It will be your turn to tell father everything we saw. Okay?"

"Yay! Thank you, Simon and Serena. Did I tell you that I love you?"

"Not yet today, Catalina," Simon laughed as he pinched his sister's cute face and received a punch in the arm similar to the one delivered to Spindle moments before.

"Why did you do that, Catalina? I didn't hurt you, did I?"

"Naw, you couldn't hurt me, Simon. That was just a love tap I gave you," Catalina looked at Spindle and giggled.

Spindle covered his face and sighed. "Oh brother. I can't believe she said that, Serena."

"Me neither." Serena gave her sister a stern face as she grunted her disapproval.

Their voices were raised now and the two camouflaged dragons stirred.

CHAPTER SIX

Evander opened his huge blue eyes and looked at the figures that stood a few feet from him and Callum. He pushed against Callum to wake him up and spoke, "Look who we have here,

Callum. We have visitors. Are you hungry?"

Callum opened his green eyes and saw the little figures standing there with opened mouths.

"What are they? They are small creatures, especially that brown one there. He is the smallest."

Spindle stepped forward pushing the three children behind him and announced in his strongest voice, "I am Spindle, a tree Sprite. I live in the trees of this land of Sovorotskina. Who are you?"

Evander let out a guttural grunt and then laughed so hard he rolled over exposing his belly.

"Do you want me to rub your belly, dragon?" Spindle asked as he moved closer.

Callum laughed at the little Sprite's candor and bravery. "You are a brave little thing, aren't you?" the dragon asked.

"Well, I try to be as brave as I can be. My father taught me to be brave in every way."

Serena stepped forward too and gripped Spindle by the arm to pull him back. "Yes, Spindle is the bravest Sprite I have ever known. He is not afraid of anything or anyone. He is my hero."

Evander sighed, "Ah, this one is also brave and she is in love with this Sprite. How sweet!"

Simon and Catalina stepped closer now to put in a good word for their sister and friend. "We are siblings and Spindle is our friend. We are not afraid of you. We have dealt with Catlings, wolves and other strange and frightening creatures before."

"Is that so?" Evander hissed as smoke came out of his mouth and drifted toward them.

When they spotted the smoke rising and coming toward them, the children, along with Spindle, moved quickly away. They weren't sure what the smoke would do to them.

"Why are you moving away, my friends? I am not going to harm you. If I wanted to, you would already be dead and eaten as our lunch. Right, Callum?"

Callum nodded but shook his head. "I would not eat you. I don't like little creatures like you. I like larger things to eat. You would not satisfy my hunger one bit and probably not taste good, especially the little stick person. I don't think we could swallow you."

"Where are you going, little ones?" Evander watched as the children slowly backed up.

Callum stressed, "I think they want to go home, Evander. Let them go. We are not supposed to get into any trouble, remember what our mistresses said."

"Oh, right. Okay. Go on your way but don't come back here or I may change my mind and eat you all," Evander let out a roar of laughter.

The children and Sprite ran the rest of the way home while Spindle sent a message to the mind of King Wizard Gateskin. A message, in return, was received immediately.

"I am on my way there, Spindle. Thank you for letting me know."

As King Gateskin was on his way to fly to rescue his children, he spotted two figures walking toward him.

"Hello there. I am Aharona and this is my sister, Navaeha. We are visiting your land and wanted to speak with you. Are you the ruler of this fine land?"

"Yes, but you must excuse me. I need to hurry off to get my children. They may be in danger."

"Danger? Are there dangerous creatures about?"

"Yes, two dragons were spotted not far from here."

"Dragons?" Aharona asked as she looked at her sister with an angry smirk. "See, I told you. Evander is getting into trouble again."

"Wait a minute. Are these dragons yours?"

"Well, um…yes. They are ours. Sorry if they caused you any trouble. They will not harm your children, I assure you. They were given a command by us to behave. They would not go back on this."

"You better come with me then to make sure my children are safe." Gateskin pulled the women up with him and flew away to find his children.

Aharona and Navaeha yelled out loud with delight when they were swooped up and carried into the wind with this powerful man.

"Wow, I didn't realize you people could fly," Aharona exclaimed.

"Only myself and my wife can do this. We are the rulers in this land of Sovorotskina. That is where you are now."

"Oh, I see. Your land is beautiful and so green. What is the stuff that is now turning brown?" Navaeha asked as they flew and finally stopped in front of a party of three children and a brown stick figure.

Gateskin did not answer Navaeha but looked at his children.

"Father, you are here! Thank goodness." Serena and her siblings rushed into his now open arms after he let the women down gently.

"I am always close by. You know I would never let anything happen to you. You are too precious to me." Gateskin sighed with a lump in his throat.

"Who are these women, Father?" Serena asked as she stepped back to look at them.

"They are the owners of the dragons you just found. This woman is Aharona and the other is her sister Navaeha. I am sure they will apologize for whatever their dragons did to frighten you."

Catalina sighed in disappointment. "I was going to tell you all about them, Father. It's not fair. I missed out again." She stomped away and sulked.

"Don't worry, little one. You can tell me all about it when we get back home." Gateskin grasped Catalina in a tight hug and kissed her on her cheeks soundly causing her to giggle.

"Okay, Father. I can't wait to explain everything to you." Looking at her siblings she said, "Don't either of you interrupt me either!"

Simon and Serena shook their heads with smirks on their faces that kept the chuckles back as they looked at their little sister's face all scrunched up and determined.

The sisters stepped forward and apologized to the children and the stick figure. "We are truly sorry if our dragons frightened you. They really are good dragons and listen to our commands. If we had not told them to behave, they may have caused you more trouble. So sorry about this to come here and cause any problems right away. We only wanted to meet you and learn more about your beautiful land," Aharona stated in a serious manner.

"Yes, we are sorry about our dragons. They really are good and kind creatures. Well, at least Callum is kinder than Evander who is fierce with everyone but me. He does have a sense of humor though," Navaeha snickered.

"We noticed that," Serena said as she smiled at them. "No harm done to any of us."

"That's a relief," Aharona smiled back at the children.

Serena introduced herself and her siblings and friend, "I am Serena. This is my brother Simon and my sister Catalina, and my best friend, Spindle. We are happy to meet you. Where did you come from?"

Aharona answered, "We are from a land far to the south of yours. It is the island of Dragonaria, Land of Dragons. We have many dragons who live there. Everyone has a dragon of their own if they want to ever fly anywhere. We do not fly on our own like your father."

Simon spoke up, "We can all fly too." He beamed.

Catalina added, "We have many powers besides that. I bet you can't guess which ones I have."

"Shh now, little one. We need to get home to your mother. She is worried about you all. Lunch is ready. You two are welcome to come to meet my wife and join us for lunch if you want."

"Oh, yes. I am starving. We were wondering where we would get something to eat. That was one of my questions," Navaeha stated as she bowed to King Gateskin in thanks.

"We are grateful for your hospitality, King Gateskin," Aharona said as she and Navaeha followed the group to the King's home.

Catalina clapped her hands and exclaimed, "I can't wait to see Mother's face when we bring home two visitors and tell her all about the dragons."

CHAPTER SEVEN

Solinara looked out the window once again for any sign of her husband and children. *Now where did they all go?*

Just as she was turning away from the window, she heard some voices. She quickly opened the door and peered out. There was her husband, children, Spindle, and two women walking at the back of the group. She watched them curiously to see if she knew these women. She shook her head. She had no recollection of ever seeing them before. Besides they were dressed differently in hoods and long brown cloaks that were cinched at their waists as if they rode animals.

Queen Fairy Solinara stepped outside to greet them and waited to hear what trouble her children had gotten into now. By the looks of Gateskin's face he was not happy and wore a puzzled expression.

"Ah, there is my beautiful queen," Gateskin announced to the two visitors as they got closer to his house. Solinara always took his breath away. He found her beauty arresting still to this day after many years of marriage. Her golden hair had a halo effect from the sun when it touched her head. He had to take a deep breath before speaking again. He knew she wouldn't be happy to hear that their children almost got eaten by two dragons. He did not look forward to being the bearer of this news. He didn't have to worry about that for too long because his youngest, Catalina, had rushed up to her mother and gleefully announced the news.

Solinara's face dropped and her eyes grew wider and fiercer as she met his gaze after hearing about the dragons from an excited Catalina.

Gateskin met her eyes, cringed inside, and cleared his throat preparing for the onslaught of emotions that would be spewed at him soon. "Solinara, the children were never in any danger per our visitors. Let me introduce them to you. This is Aharona and her sister Navaeha. They come from a faraway island called Dragonaria, Land of Dragons."

The Queen gained her composure in a flash and smiled at the women reaching out to take their hands and welcome them to her home. "It is a pleasure to meet you both. You must be tired coming from such a long journey. How did you get here?"

"We rode our dragons. That is why your children stumbled upon them in the woods. We must assure you, as King Gateskin said, the children were never in any danger of being harmed. Our dragons are well behaved and would not hurt anyone unless our lives were threatened," Aharona announced, observing the amazing composure of the Queen.

"I see. I thank you for that. I hope your dragons will not get into any trouble out there in the woods. There are a lot of people who may also take that path and run into them."

Navaeha reacted, "Evander who is my dragon, and Callum is Aharona's dragon, are well behaved and were instructed by us to not get into any trouble or harm anyone. They know that we would not be happy with them if they disobeyed us."

"You make them sound like children who behave when you instruct them to do so," Solinara said with a tight smile.

"Well, I guess they are like our children. I have known Evander since I was just three years old. He adopted me," Navaeha said with a snicker. She looked at her sister and winked.

"I certainly hope you are correct in saying that, ladies. But what if a Catling comes along? Would they attack it?" Solinara met their eyes to see if they were sincere.

"Catling? Is that what they call those large cats?"

"Yes, have you already met one?" Solinara asked, surprised they lived to talk about it.

"Unfortunately, in the deeper part of the forest we almost landed on a few of them feasting," Aharona added.

Gateskin joined in and said, "Yes, you must have been in their territory called the Unknown Territory or the UT. We still call it that even though it is well known now to all of us."

"It was quite dark and heavily forested and not at all a safe place to stay. Can I ask you a question, King Gateskin?" Aharona queried.

"Of course, what is it?"

"Well, when we were flying overhead and spotted this land mass, we noticed how green it was all over and then suddenly the green which appeared to be moving stopped and began to turn brown. What was that?"

"That is not easily explained. What do you know about our land?"

The sisters exchanged guarded looks before Aharona responded, "The only thing we know is that there was the Medallion lost somewhere around here. We had heard stories from a Wizard who passed through our villages. My sister and I wanted to see if we could find it. We love mysteries and thought it would be fun to do this. There is not much happening on our island. Our father keeps us close and never lets us out of his sight."

"He may come looking for you then if you do not go back home soon," Gateskin announced in alarm.

"I don't think so. We told him we were just going for a little ride around and would return later for supper. He shouldn't be looking for us unless we don't show up to eat."

Solinara quickly prepared two more sandwiches and set them out in front of everyone as she brewed some of her special tea. She shared her thoughts with Gateskin in his mind. "I don't know how much we can tell these newcomers about our land. Be careful. They could be spies for King Kaposkaran."

King Kaposkaran and Queen Beregina are rulers of the land of Parotovina. They were not to be trusted since they had tried several times to send spies to Sovorotskina to undermine the King Gateskin's power.

"Yes, I agree, Solinara. We can never be too careful."

Queen Solinara set the tea on the table and poured tea for their visitors, keeping an eye on them while staying in tune with Gateskin.

Gateskin and Solinara did not share anything with the visitors, instead they asked them to talk about their homeland.

The children, powerful in their own ways, discussed amongst themselves what they thought their parents were thinking about the visitors. They weren't sure if they should say anything at all themselves.

Time would tell all.

CHAPTER EIGHT

After finishing lunch and discussing their island, the sisters excused themselves and pushed away from the table. "Thank you so much, Queen Solinara, for the delicious lunch. The tea was wonderful too. I would love to know what kind it is," Navaeha stated, with a smile.

"You are most welcome, ladies. I prepare my own brew. I can give you some of the tea leaves to take with you."

"I look forward to having more soon. Our mother will love it too."

"Navaeha, we cannot tell Mother or Father about our little adventure here. It would not be safe for any of us."

"Right. Father would want to meet King Gateskin to make sure he did not harm us in any way."

"Harm you? Why would I harm you?" Gateskin asked in alarm.

Solinara turned back from the sink where she was washing the dishes and asked, "Why would he think that, ladies? That is a terrible thing to say."

"Oh, we did not want to insult you for all you have done for us to make us feel welcome in your home. We are truly sorry," Aharona quickly added.

"Maybe it is time for you to leave," Solinara announced briskly as she opened the door for them.

"We are sorry for hurting your feelings. We had no intention of doing that. You are both most gracious, and King Gateskin is a true gentleman. No worries please. We will not even mention where we have been. Can we come back again and learn more about your land as you now know more about ours?" Navaeha asked meekly.

"Maybe another time, but not too soon. We will think about it," Gateskin stated as he met his wife's glare. "Let me walk you back to your dragons. I would like to see them closeup for myself.

He nodded to his wife and stepped outside.

"Can we go with Father too?" Catalina asked in anticipation.

"No, you may not. Go to your rooms. I will be there shortly to discuss your adventure in more detail."

"Yes, Mother," the three children responded reluctantly and trudged to their prospective rooms, but soon gathered in Serena's.

Solinara watched her husband walk back through the woods and sent him a message, "Be careful, my love. Come back right away. We have much to discuss."

Gateskin looked up and nodded as he responded, "Yes, my queen. I promise to do that."

The children were having their own discussions in Serena's room through their shared mind transfers, to be as quiet as possible.

Catalina was the first to speak, "What do you think Mother will do to Father?"

"Nothing, Catalina. She wanted Father to know she wasn't happy and they would have more to discuss as soon as he came back."

"How do you know that, Serena?" Simon asked, perplexed that his sister knew something he didn't.

"I use my intuition, and the look on Mother's face tells me a lot."

"Hmm, I still don't get it!"

"I use my intuition too, Serena," Catalina added with a smirk.

Simon gave Catalina a growl and stuck his tongue out at her. Catalina responded in kind which brought them both to giggles.

The giggles soon quieted down as their mother peeked into their rooms and told them to come with her. The children followed her to the family room and were told to sit down.

They did as they were told and folded their hands on their laps as they waited to hear what their mother would say to them. By the expression on her face, it wouldn't be too bad. She was even wearing a smile now.

"Now, please tell me in detail all about these dragons. What colors were they and how large? Were they fierce or quiet? Did they send smoke out to you or fire?"

Catalina jumped up and down and responded before her siblings could get their bearings. "Yes, mother, one did send smoke to us but we backed away from it in case it would harm us."

"Good thinking, Catalina. The smoke is there before the fire and can put you to sleep before you even know it. This is how they devour their prey and eat them unawares. I guess it is a way to do this without causing the prey any pain."

"Oh, no! We could have been eaten even if the ladies said otherwise. Right, Mother?"

"Yes, that is quite possible. I am relieved that you thought carefully about getting too close to them. It could have been that the dragons just wanted to frighten you. They were given a command and could not cross over from that."

"Do you want to know what colors they were, Mother?" Simon asked, ready to jump into the conversation.

"Of course."

"Well, one was blue and gold and was quite fierce. He is the one who sent smoke over to us."

Serena picked up the conversation next, "The second one was multi-colored like a rainbow and was a kinder and quieter one. He even told the mean dragon to be careful and not to harm us. I don't think he would have eaten us anyway. Maybe the first one was just being a bully, and the kind one knew that, and reined him in."

"You may be right, Serena. It certainly sounds that way. Thank goodness for the kind one. From what the ladies said, it sounds like the kind one is called Callum and the fierce one is Evander."

"I like those names, Mother. I wish we had a dragon too," Catalina sighed.

"What would you do with it, Catalina? It would probably eat all our livestock and wolves and whatever else it could find."

"Oh, no, not our livestock and wolves. They are our friends. I don't mind if the dragon ate a Catling or two. That's okay," Catalina sighed, then giggled at the thought. "I guess we would have to build a shelter for all our animals to keep them safe and tell the dragon not to harm any of them or else," Catalina announced.

"Or else what, Catalina?" Simon asked as he shook his head in disbelief at his sister's naivete.

"How would we get a dragon, Mother?" Serena asked, inquisitively.

"There are no dragons here on our land. May be at one time there were. It sounds like they are all on Dragonaria where the ladies came from for now. It is possible the dragons and their riders will be back. They are determined to find the Medallion. Do you remember the story I told you about the Medallion?"

"Yes, I remember," Serena said as she exchanged glances with her siblings.

"I do too," Simon responded in kind.

"I don't remember, Mother. Can you tell me about it? Maybe I was too young at the time," Catalina replied with eyes full of curiosity.

"Well, okay. Let's see. Many years ago, long before either your father or I were born, an evil Wizard came to Sovorotskina to find a Medallion that he said his father had buried here. He visited all the farms and dug up their areas to no avail. It was never found. This Wizard put a spell on the people who lived at that time and made their farms stop producing any crops until someone came forward to tell him where the Medallion was. He vowed to return to continue his search."

"What happened to the people? Did they starve?" Simon asked in shock, not remembering this part of the story.

"No, another Wizard came along and took off the spell and continued to look for the Medallion. He believed the people that they did not know where it was. I guess I never shared the rest of the story with you."

"What kind of Medallion was it?" Serena asked, waiting with eager anticipation.

"Supposedly it was gold and had a magical quality to it that would make the bearer powerful as a Wizard or even more powerful if the bearer was already a Wizard."

"Maybe Father can find this Medallion and become more powerful than any Wizard ever was," Catalina exclaimed with enthusiasm.

"No, I don't think your father would want that. He is the most powerful Wizard on this land. He doesn't need any more power. Your father is a kind and caring ruler. He would never use something like that to his own benefit. If he ever found it, he would destroy it to prevent anyone from using it adversely."

"What does that mean, Mother, adversely?" Catalina asked in confusion.

"Well, it means against others to cause them harm."

"I understand. Thank you, Mother. I am not used to larger words like that. But I will learn soon. I am getting more grown up every day."

"Yes, I can see that, Catalina. I am proud of you and your siblings. You are all very brave, intelligent, and powerful too. You need to use your powers for good. Always remember that. If you had to protect yourself against the dragons you could have used it then. Do you know what you would have done to protect yourself if you were in danger from the dragons?"

Serena spoke up, "Yes, I would have put a spell on them to stop them from moving and give us time to run away."

"That would have worked for a time, but not for long."

"Okay, then I would have put them to sleep with a spell and moved them far away from us," Serena quickly added.

"Good one, Serena. What about you, Simon? What would you do?"

"I would fly us out of there so fast that they would only see a blur as we moved away."

"Okay. That is good too. What about you Catalina?"

"I would make us all invisible and blend into our surroundings."

"Can you do that to others too, Catalina?" Solinara asked, clearly surprised.

"Well, I have been working on it. I picked up my toys and made them disappear with me the other day. I think I can do that with my brother and sister too."

"That is impressive, little one. I must see you do that sometime," Solinara stated with pride.

"Well, I think we have had enough discussion about this subject for today. I need to speak further with your father. Stay close to the house and away from the woods. I don't know if our visitors have left yet."

"Yes, Mother. We'll go visit the wolves. We haven't seen the cubs for a while. They are growing quite large now and not cubs anymore," Serena announced. "Don't worry, Mother, about us. I will watch over Simon and Catalina. I promise."

"Thank you, Serena. I know I can trust you. Be careful now with the wolves. Maybe you should feed them first before you go play with them."

"We will. Mother."

Solinara sighed and watched for her husband to return.

CHAPTER NINE

Out in the woods Gateskin was meeting the dragons who were now awake, alert, and waiting for their mistresses to bring them a treat.

Aharona looked at Navaeha. "We didn't bring them treats like we promised if they were good. What do we do now? They won't be happy with us."

"Oops, that's right. I forgot."

"What's wrong, ladies?" Gateskin stood behind them, listening as he looked over their heads at the dragons who were looking back at him with curiosity.

"We promised our dragons to bring them some treats if they behaved themselves," Navaeha responded.

"Oh, I see. What about this?" Gateskin pulled out of thin air two large furry creatures and placed them in front of the dragons whose eyes grew wide in delight. They quickly gobbled up the creatures and smiled. Burps were soon heard as they digested their prey.

"How did you do that, King Gateskin?" Aharona asked with wide eyes of her own.

"Well, I do have some powers that I use when needed."

"I guess you do. That was amazing! What else can you do?" Navaeha asked, eagerly.

"I only use my powers when absolutely necessary. But I can send you off on your journey with a brisk wind to help you get home quicker."

"Can you do that? That would be most helpful since we may arrive a little later than we expected. Time went by so quickly," Aharona exclaimed with relief.

"Most certainly I can. I don't want your father to come looking for you here," Gateskin stated, with a smirk.

"We hope you will apologize for us again to your lovely wife. We are so sorry to upset her. We would love to come back here another day to learn more about your land. We find it all fascinating, don't we, Navaeha?"

"Yes, we do. We also want to hear more about the Medallion and its background, how it came to be here and never found."

"Well, I don't know a lot about the Medallion or why it came here but maybe another time when you come. I will also speak to my wife. I know she can be strong about protecting our family as I am. We don't want any trouble from your island or more people coming here. Please do not share any of this with your people. There are other rulers here that would not accept any visitors as kindly as I do. It could be most dangerous for you or any others who come back. There is much you do not know about our lands here."

"Now you have piqued our interest even more, Gateskin. We could protect ourselves and you and your family too if you ever need us. Remember, we have powerful dragons at our disposal. There are numerous ones on our island yet to be tamed if you ever need one."

"I don't think we will, but thank you just the same. If I ever need you, I will send you a message somehow."

"How will you do that?" Aharona asked, clearly mystified.

"I would find a way. You will know it is me because I will say, 'come back to Sovorotskina right away.'"

"Okay, well, it was a pleasure to meet you. We should introduce you to our dragons. Come a little closer. They will not harm you especially after that treat you gave them," Navaeha said with a giggle.

"In fact, I think you just made two friends for life," Aharona added with a wink.

"I am relieved to hear that. If you are sure, I would be happy to meet them. I have never met a dragon face-to-face before," Gateskin chuckled.

"This colorful devil is mine. His name is Evander." Turning to her dragon Navaeha said, "Evander, meet King Gateskin who is a Wizard and the one who gave you that delicious treat. Bow to him, please."

Evander stood up and bowed, showing off his colorful scales that glistened in the light that streamed over him. He opened his huge blue eyes and winked at Gateskin.

"My pleasure to meet you, Evander," King Gateskin bowed back at the dragon and gave him his own wink.

Aharona stepped forward and introduced her dragon. "This sweetheart is my dragon, also colorful. His name is Callum. He is a kind and endearing dragon, one of a kind. Turning to her dragon she said,

"Callum, this is King Wizard Gateskin, the one who gave you that treat too."

Callum bowed down and flexed his sparkling, multi-colored wings in tribute to the King.

Gateskin bowed back at him too and lightly touched Callum's colorful wing that spread out in front of him making the dragon purr like a kitten.

"I think you made four new friends, King Gateskin, us, and our dragons. We look forward to meeting again sometime." Aharona bowed to King Gateskin.

"Safe travels, Aharona and Navaeha. Be careful and fly high and away from here. I don't want anyone to see you."

"Well, that would be hard to do. How do we disappear?" Navaeha asked.

"I will put you under a spell until you leave our borders then it will wear off and you will be on your way without any problems."

"Thank you, kind king. We wish you and your family well. Your wife is beautiful and your children delightful. We look forward to seeing you all again," Aharona said as she and her sister waved and flew away under King Gateskin's Disappearing Spell.

Gateskin turned away after assuring that they were gone and beyond the borders of Noella Province. He headed back home as quickly as he could. He knew his wife would be anxiously awaiting his return and would have more questions and concerns she needed to voice.

He was unaware that others had seen these dragons and there would be questions asked of him and answers expected soon.

CHAPTER TEN

As Gateskin headed back to his home two people jumped out of the bushes and cornered him.

"Gateskin, who and what was that?" Wizard Hotenfaran, his brother-in-law asked as he brushed off the leaves from his cloak that were there from his hiding place.

Fairy Procelina, Hotenfaran's wife, came alongside him and raised her brows, waiting for an answer.

"Ah, I thought I felt someone close by following me. I should have known it was you two. You are quite stealthy." Gateskin met them with a hug and pat on their backs.

"Did we frighten you, King?" Procelina asked in concern.

"Oh no. It would take quite a bit more than that to frighten me."

"Well, are you going to share what that was all about - the visitors and their magnificent dragons?"

"It's good to see you both too!" Gateskin snickered.

"Oh, yes, of course, it is always good to see you, my king," Hotenfaran responded, with a smirk and bowed in reverence.

"Sorry, King Gateskin. We did not mean to be disrespectful!" Procelina added, quickly.

"I am only joking with you both. It is always good to see you. I have been busy entertaining two guests who came from the island of Dragonaria, Land of Dragons."

"Yes, we saw the dragons. They were incredible! They took my breath away!" Procelina exclaimed with a deep sigh. "Are they coming back?"

"That I don't know. I think they want to come back. But I don't think their father will take too kindly to them traveling such a distance with the possible dangers they may encounter."

"Hmm, I would feel the same about my child, Gateskin. Since we became parents all I can think of is our son,

Arubane, and protecting him from any dangers."

"Yes, that is what parenthood does to you. I know that three times over. I never stop worrying about my children either. But I think that is part of being a good parent. You two are the best."

"Thank you, my king. So, please continue. Tell us about these visitors and why they came here," Hotenfaran pleaded.

"Well, it seems that they are interested in the missing Medallion on our land."

"The Medallion? Why would they be interested after all this time? Who told them about it?" Procelina quizzed.

"They said a Wizard passed through their village and mentioned it a long time ago. The message is still clear to many there and the two sisters, Aharona and Navaeha, are determined to find it."

"I see. This could spell trouble for us, Gateskin," Hotenfaran stated, with a furrowed brow. "I don't like it."

"I don't either, Hotenfaran. There is nothing to do now. When they return home, their father will be upset with them for traveling so far away and most likely will not let them out of his sight again."

"Do you think that will stop these two women from venturing out again?"

"No, I do not. I am expecting a visit from them again soon. I only hope they do not share this quest with anyone else on their island or we will be inundated with visitors carrying shovels."

"Oh boy! That is not a good thing. We will keep watch for the dragons. They can't hide from me, Gateskin," Procelina said with a smile.

"That I can be sure of, Procelina. You have the keenest eyes of anyone and can see far and wide. Nothing can get past your vision."

"That is my wife, eagle eyes I call her," Hotenfaran said with a guffaw which caused his wife to punch him playfully on the arm.

Hotenfaran met her eyes with love and gave her a hug in return.

Gateskin cleared his throat and said, "Sorry to break up this lovefest, but I need to get back to my wife. She will want a full report on what transpired with these two ladies and their pets. She wasn't at all happy with them. She kicked them out and told them not to come back."

"What? My sister said that? I don't believe it!" Hotenfaran said with a deep chuckle.

"Good for her, Gateskin. What did they do to warrant that?" Procelina asked.

"Well, maybe she will explain it to you sometime. Now I am going to be in trouble if I don't get back to her pronto."

"Go on your way, King," Hotenfaran said. "I know what a temper my sister has if she is not pleased with me. I wouldn't want to change places with you."

"Good luck, my king," Procelina giggled as she took her husband's arm and marched back home to their son, Arubane who would be thrilled to hear about the dragons.

CHAPTER ELEVEN

Solinara paced back and forth and kept looking out the window for Gateskin. She was getting worried by the minute. He was taking entirely too long to get back.

She looked up when she heard the door open and saw her dashing husband standing there with a smirk on his face.

"I was wondering when you would get back. I was beginning to think that the dragons…"

"Don't go there, Solinara. You know I can take care of any situation. In fact, I made four new friends today."

"Four?"

"Well, four if you count the sisters and their dragons."

"Now they are your friends after what they said about you? How could you feel that way? I was insulted."

"I know. They told me to extend their apologies to you again. They feel terrible about what they said."

"I guess I overreacted a little but it still wasn't nice to say about my husband harming them in any way. You are a gentleman and a sweet man who wouldn't harm a hair on their heads even if they caused us some trouble."

"That is true. But I will keep an eye on them when they come back."

"Come back? They are returning? Why?" Solinara's brows knitted in concern.

"Don't worry, my love. They will not be a problem. I warned them to keep everything quiet about our province. I also told them of the dangers of the other lands here and their rulers, that they wouldn't be as welcome there as they were here."

"Were the dragons fierce, Gateskin?"

"Not at all. They were eating out of my hands." He chuckled as he saw his wife's shocked expression.

"Did you feed them?"

"As a matter of fact, I did. I gave them a treat since their mistresses forgot to bring one back for them for their good behavior."

"Did they try to bite you?"

"Oh, no. In fact, when I touched Callum's wing he purred like a kitten."

"Really? That is amazing. I didn't know that dragons could be so tame."

"Next time they come I will have them introduce you to their dragons, Evander and Callum."

"Interesting names. I like them. I look forward to meeting them only if the sisters behave themselves and treat you with respect."

"Don't worry, sweetheart. They already do. Now, where are our children? I hope they are not in more trouble."

"In fact, they are in their rooms right now. That is where I sent them to think over what they did by straying too close to the dragons and strangers."

"I think I will go see if they have repented yet," Gateskin said with a snicker.

Gateskin peeked into his oldest daughter's room and found it empty. He next went to his son's room and found that empty too. He stood outside his youngest daughter's room and waited until the three looked up at him. They were deep in conversation with one another as they sat on Catalina's bed.

"Father! We were wondering when you would come back. What happened to the sisters and their dragons?" Serena asked as she exchanged glances with her siblings.

"You might enjoy this little story about the dragons," Gateskin said with a smile and a wink.

"Please tell us, Father," Catalina begged.

"Well, it seems that these dragons are like kittens and they purr just like one."

"Purr like a kitten? I didn't know they could do that or even want to, Father," Simon responded with wonder.

"What happened, Father?" Serena probed.

Gateskin then explained how he gave each dragon a furry treat out of midair.

"Wow, that is so cool, Father. I wish we could have been there. Will they come back to visit again? I hope so!" Simon exclaimed with wide eyes.

"I'm not sure. But maybe they will. I don't know when though. If they do come back, I do not want any of you going near the dragons again. Do you hear me?"

"Yes, Father. We promise," Serena stated as she met her siblings with a glare.

"I will depend on you, Serena, to make sure they do not. I do not want to worry about any of you being eaten as a snack."

"Oh, Father! The dragons wouldn't eat us. They like us! I could tell by their eyes. They have kind eyes or at least Callum does. Evander is a little unsure of what to do with us, but I think he likes us."

"You can never be too sure about dragons. They can turn on you unless you are their mistress or master."

"Can we have a dragon, Father?" Simon asked.

"No, absolutely not. We do not have any room for dragons here in Noella Province. What would we feed them?"

"We could feed them Catlings, Father," Simon suggested.

"Maybe we could have Mother make some more food for them to have. She could come up with a new special dragon food with Uncle Hotenfaran's help. They can do wonderful things like that together," Serena proposed.

"Yes, I agree, Father," Simon added.

"I don't think I would ask your mother about that yet. She is still unhappy about the visitors and wouldn't be open to any of your suggestions at the moment. It is best to stay clear of your mother's wrath for now."

"Is she still angry with the sisters?" Serena asked timidly.

"I'm afraid so, honey. I am staying low myself around her until she is calmer. I would suggest you all do whatever she asks of you and keep your rooms clean, set the table and whatever else."

"Yes, Father. We will do that. We don't want Mother to be angry with us," Serena agreed.

Simon added, "I will go see what Mother needs for me to do right now. That will make her happy, right, Father?"

"I think it will, Simon. Did you feed the animals today?"

"Yes, I fed the chickens, horse, cow, and goats. I can go feed the wolves now too. Come with me, Serena, in case I must converse with them. You too, Catalina. I may also need your expertise."

Catalina smiled at being included, hopped off her bed and followed her siblings outside.

Her father winked and patted her on the head as she passed by him bringing a sweet smile to her lips and a sparkle to her eyes as Catalina winked back.

CHAPTER TWELVE

Serena was busy in the kitchen preparing dinner ahead of time. She was making a special dinner for her husband to show that she was not angry with him anymore.

She watched their children from the kitchen window feed the wolves and play with the new cubs that were just birthed, adding to the growing wolf population.

She felt her husband's arm encircle her waist as she lay her head against him and sighed happily.

"What are you making, my love?" Gateskin asked in curiosity.

"It is a surprise, sweetheart. I will let you know when it is ready, Gateskin."

"Ooh, I like surprises that smell this delicious! I can't wait!" He planted a kiss on her cheek and went outside to join the children and check on the other animals.

Gateskin watched from a distance as the wolf cubs happily sat in the children's laps as they received much love and attention. He chuckled as he saw the look on Catalina's face of such adoration as she petted one of the new cubs.

Catalina looked up when she saw her father walking toward them. "Aren't they cute, Father?"

"Yes, they are, Catalina. But remember they will grow quite large and won't be as cute when full grown."

"I still will love them, Father. They love me back; don't you see that?"

"Yes, I guess I do, sweetheart. Who wouldn't love you?" he said with a broad smile and a heart full of love.

"Thank you, Father. They understand what we say when I talk to them and they send messages back to me that they are happy here."

"I'm glad to hear that. We wouldn't want unhappy wolves at our door," he guffawed.

Simon listened and added, "I can't understand them but I can see they are happy with their lives here and love the food that Mother and Uncle Hotenfaran created for them."

"You should share that with your mother. She would like to hear that the wolves enjoy her food. She will want to make a lot more."

"Maybe she should be making more since the wolf population is growing much larger. What are we going to do if we have too many of them, Father?" Serena stated with concern.

"I haven't given that much thought, Serena. I guess we may have to find more room for them somewhere and build some more huts too."

"Do you want us to build some huts, Father?" Simon asked with eagerness. He was always looking for something new to do.

"Let me think this over, Simon, and I will let you know. Okay?"

"Sure," Simon responded in disappointment.

"Don't look so sad. I promise to let you know when and if we need more. You will be the first one to know."

"Okay, Father. Thank you." Simon went back to feeding and petting the new cubs.

Serena was concentrating on the mother wolf as she appeared to be conversing with her. Simon watched in envy.

"I wish I could do that like you and Catalina."

"Do what, Simon?" Serena looked up at her brother in confusion.

"Well, you are speaking with the wolf, aren't you?"

"Yes, in fact, I was. The mother wolf asked me if I would get some more food for her since she is still hungry and may be pregnant again."

"Oh wow! That means Father will have to approve more huts. Maybe you should tell him this, Serena, to convince him sooner to enlist me to begin building more."

"I can help you, Simon," Catalina added with enthusiasm.

"Maybe Father will make up his mind sooner."

"I can be a big help to you, Simon," Catalina responded again with gusto.

Serena watched her siblings walk away to find their father who was in the barn with the animals. She giggled to herself as she pictured her brother and sister working together to build huts. It would be quite a sight and an earful that she would see and hear. She would stay clear as they attempted to do this, for she wanted no part in helping them. She knew how they would argue about every detail.

She nodded to the mother wolf and went to her mother's and uncle's workshop to pick up some more food for the hungry mother wolf. She didn't want the wolf to eat her own cubs if she was so inclined. Serena gave a shiver just to think of this.

She searched around and found a large bag of food and scooped out some in a bowl to give to the mother wolf. She would make sure that her mother knew that the supply of wolf food was getting low.

Roaming around the edges of the woods that bordered the wolves' huts were hungry Catlings unbeknownst to anyone in Sovorotskina. The Catlings watched as the many new cubs got closer to the borders causing the

Catlings to salivate and soak the ground around them.

CHAPTER THIRTEEN

Back on the island of Dragonaria the sisters were being carefully watched after their confrontation with their parents about their long absence. Aharona and Navaeha tried not to share too much with their parents for fear there would be reprisals that would fall on King Wizard Gateskin preventing them from ever returning there.

They told their parents instead that they had just taken a long ride around and forgot about the time and didn't realize how far they had traveled.

Their parents had met their explanation with some hesitancy and doubt but didn't question them any further. The girls were told that they were not to leave the island for the time being and would have to keep their dragons tied down until otherwise given the word that they could use them again.

"I can't believe this, Aharona! They don't trust us!"

"I know, I am not at all happy with their decision either, sister. Maybe we should have shared a little about our trip to…" Navaeha sighed heavily and grumbled her discontent.

"Shh, don't even say it! Someone might hear us and tell our parents. Then we would be grounded forever!" Aharona exclaimed as she looked around for anyone skulking close by.

The dragons lounged around not able to move very far from their tethers. They snorted and roared unhappily.

"Aharona, we can't keep them tied down. It is not fair to them. They need to move around. Why can't we let them go? They will come back if we call them."

"I agree. It is inhumane or should I say inhumane to dragons to do this. They need to move around like we do. I am getting restless too. I know how they feel," Aharona sighed.

She pulled out the stakes holding the dragons and whispered to them, "Don't go anywhere near our parents or they will tether you again. Stay close though, in case we need you. Don't worry, we will travel together soon." Aharona patted the dragons and let them fly away.

"Father will see them flying away, Aharona. They are quite distinguishable from any of the other dragons."

"I know, but Father is too busy in his meeting now and Mother won't even look up. She is always involved with some project."

"You're right. Okay, I will relax," Navaeha let out a sigh of relief.

"Let's think about a way to escape again, sister," Aharona stated as she wore a look of intense concentration.

"I'm always thinking about doing something. You know me," Navaeha replied equally in deep thought.

Aharona added, "I really want to go back to you know where. I think we should try to convince them that they need us as friends and that we are invaluable to them, especially with our dragons. Callum and Evander really liked the lands there. They told me so."

"Yes, Evander shared that with me too. He said he wanted to go visit his new friend who gave them the delicious snack. He wants to have some more. They were evidently quite tasty and habit forming." Navaeha looked up to see if she could spot her dragon in the sky.

"Don't worry about them. They won't go too far and will stay away from Father. They know him well," Aharona stated as she lay down on the mats outside their huts and stretched in the warm sun.

The sisters were given their own huts to sleep in or do whatever they wanted in privacy. They had earned that privilege when they proved they were old enough to be on their own. They did not want to lose that privilege by disobeying their parents now that they were seventeen and eighteen.

"You should be able to do whatever you want since you are eighteen, Aharona," her sister stated, with a grimace. "I will be old enough next year and hope they will give me more room to move around also."

"I don't think Father thinks that way. Maybe we have to prove that we can be trustworthy by staying out of trouble more. He is still upset about the other incidents in the past."

"Oh, right. You mean when we took the dragons and hid with them behind the falls."

"Yes, and the other time that we stole some of the chickens to feed the dragons."

"Yeah, that too. I guess we need to stay low for a while until he cools off."

"Those were fun times, weren't they, Navaeha?" her sister giggled.

"It's always fun with you, Aharona, but trouble seems to follow us. I wonder why?" Navaeha laughed out loud and quickly covered her mouth when she saw someone walking by and staring at them.

"Who was that?" Aharona asked as she kept looking at the figure moving away from them.

"It's probably that girl who hates us. We got her into trouble when she used to hang around with us."

Aharona whispered, "Oh, you mean, Mianna? Yes, I think that was she. Did you notice she didn't look happy to see us in a good mood."

"I don't think she has forgiven you for getting her into trouble with her father. She wasn't supposed to go with us to the falls that day when we hid with the dragons. She nearly drowned trying to go under the falls with us." Navaeha kept watch to see if Mianna was still around.

"I know! I was frightened half to death when I pulled her out and brought her back home to her parents. She looked like a drowned rat!" Aharona guffawed but then muffled herself.

"Maybe we have to grow up a little sister," Navaeha responded, with a serious expression that soon turned into a snicker.

"Wow! I was wondering if you were serious there for a minute," Aharona said as she punched her sister playfully in the arm.

"Haha. Right!" Navaeha laughed.

Aharona sat up and looked around. "Did you hear something?"

"What? I didn't hear anything." Navaeha looked around and concentrated.

"Listen. I think King Gateskin is calling us."

"What? How? Is he here?" Navaeha asked in surprise.

"Remember he told us that when he needed our help, he would summon us. He didn't say how but that we would know it when we heard it."

"Seriously, Aharona? I didn't hear anything." Navaeha stood up and listened again.

"He just said, 'Come to Sovorotskina now! You are needed.' Maybe it has something to do with those cat-like creatures. What did they call them?"

"Oh, I remember. They said they were Catlings," Navaeha responded.

"Yes, that's what they are. We need to go back there. We better call our dragons and see if we can go quickly before Father is out of his meeting."

"Are you sure we can do this, Aharona? I don't know if we can get away again so soon."

"Don't worry, I will come up with something." Aharona turned and whispered to summon their dragons - a command only they could hear.

Hiding behind their huts was their cousin, Jelitza, who planned to find out where they were going.

CHAPTER FOURTEEN

Back in Sovorotskina King Gateskin mulled over the situation with the encroaching Catlings. He decided after conferring with the Wizards, even after they promised to create more and more powerful spells, that he couldn't trust just the spells to keep these creatures at bay. He had to turn elsewhere for help.

He created another spell using his Channel Spell to contact the sisters and their dragons. He sent this message: "Come to Sovorotskina now! You are needed!"

He waited to see if this message went through the Channel Spell window. He opened it up and looked through to see if he could decipher if the sisters were on their way. He saw the Sea of Shakelle which was rough as it always was as if it were an angry serpent ready to strike anyone who dared to venture upon it.

He searched the skies and finally spotted two dots on the horizon that were slowly growing. He kept his focus on the dots as they became giant wings that beat the air with a frantic tempo. He sighed in relief that this new Message Spell worked.

***

"I can hear the message now from King Wizard Gateskin. It is getting louder the closer we get to his village in Noella Province. I wonder why I couldn't hear it when we were home like you did, Aharona."

"I did hear the message and felt the vibrations. He promised he would get in touch with us and when we felt it, we would know."

"Yes, I do remember him saying that," Navaeha replied as she watched the landscape of Noella Province suddenly come into view.

"It is so beautiful here, isn't it, Navaeha? We seemed to be arriving sooner than last time. I guess we know our way better now."

"Oh, yes, sister. I do love this land. Though our island is beautiful too. But there is something different about this place. It holds much mystery to me too. I agree, we did arrive quicker this time."

"Yes, maybe we will live here one day," Aharona sighed as she whispered to Callum to land in a safer place than they did last time. She didn't want to see those vile creatures again.

"Why do you think King Gateskin needs us, Aharona, if it is not the Catlings?"

"We will find out soon enough, Navaeha. Look down there; it's King Gateskin. He is waving at us to land near him."

"That is strange. I thought he didn't want us to come too close to his home. What will his wife say about our visiting again so soon?"

"I don't know, but I'm sure he will tell us. Let's keep quiet until he is finished explaining why we were summoned." Aharona looked at her sister with a serious expression.

"Don't look at me that way, Aharona. I will keep quiet. I promise." Navaeha zipped her lips and tried not to smirk.

Gateskin stepped away to let the dragons' land. When Evander and Callum spotted the King, they began to drool, anticipating another tasty treat.

The King stepped closer with two furry creatures in his hands and put them at the feet of the dragons who quickly gobbled them up making plenty of smacking noises of enjoyment for all to hear.

"I can't believe you two!" Aharona exclaimed. "You are very rude to King Gateskin. What do you say to him for these treats? You didn't even greet him first."

Callum bowed his head and Evander did the same and crawled closer to Gateskin to lick his feet in thanks.

Gateskin chuckled to see these huge creatures at his feet bowing before him. "I take it that you two liked the treats I gave you. Don't worry I will make more for you soon. You are most welcome." The King bowed back to them and turned his attention to the sisters.

"I imagine that you are wondering why I called you back so soon."

"Well, yes, in fact we were puzzled, King Gateskin," Aharona said, and poked her sister to keep quiet. Navaeha moved further away from her sister so she couldn't be punched again.

"Come with me," Gateskin announced as he walked briskly away and added, "You can leave the dragons there. They will be fine until we return."

"Okay," the sisters replied in unison.

"Callum and Evander, you need to stay here and remember to behave yourselves. We will return soon. Take a nap. I'm sure you are tired after the long ride and now full from the treats."

The dragons nodded and laid their heads down on their legs, fell asleep and disappeared under the cover of their camouflage.

"Wow, did you see that? I wish I could go to sleep so fast, Aharona."

"I know, sister, so do I. I also wish I could disappear like that."

"Where is the King taking us, Aharona?"

"Be patient, Navaeha. I don't know why you have to know everything instantly. Just wait a little longer and enjoy our surroundings. It is so beautiful with all these forests around us. Everything's so green and smells woodsy and minty at the same time."

"Hmm, I noticed that too. I could take a bath in this grass. It tickles my ankles."

King Gateskin raised his hand up to the sisters to stop. He turned to look at them and put his finger up to his lips to be quiet.

The sounds they heard were not human but something only a creature that was out of this world could make and not something they wanted to meet right now.

CHAPTER FIFTEEN

"What was that, King Gateskin?" Aharona asked as her sister hugged her side for protection.

"That is what we call Catlings. They are the reason I summoned you both here today. We have a problem with them trying to breach our borders from their own in the Unknown Territory."

"Oh, right. The Unknown Territory or UT is where we landed when we first came here. We saw those horrible creatures who would have eaten us for a snack if we didn't have our dragons with us. I think they were frightened by Callum and Evander."

"Yes, that is why I need you here today to help deter the invasion of these creatures again."

"Again? They came here before?" Navaeha responded and quickly shut her mouth after seeing her sister's stern face of disapproval.

"It's okay for her to ask me that, Aharona. No worries. I plan to explain everything. Yes, they did come here to all of Noella Province but mostly to Parotovina where they nearly decimated all the livestock in the village before being stopped by the Moss Spell.

"A moss spell?" Navaeha asked as she avoided looking at her sister.

Gateskin explained about the Moss Spell, who created it, how it worked, and how the creatures had to be taken out of the village once they fell asleep after ingesting it and were brought back to the Unknown Territory.

"Wow! That is incredible!" Why do the creatures want to come here now?" Aharona asked.

"It appears that they have decimated the food supply of their own land and are now starving. They have tried to cross over my border around where I keep the wolves and their cubs. I was fortunate that I was feeding the cubs along with my children when I noticed the Catlings roaming back and forth through the copse behind the wolf huts. They nearly caught two cubs who were wandering too close to the border there."

"I would love to see these wolves!" Navaeha announced with wide-eyed wonder.

"Yes, I thought you might," Gateskin laughed at Navaeha's exuberance. "Come this way."

Aharona poked her sister and whispered, "You didn't have to interrupt like that. I wanted to hear more about the spells and how they worked."

"Plenty of time for that, sister. Now, let's see these wolves. They are more fascinating to me than some old spells."

Aharona sighed and followed her sister and King Gateskin.

When the three had arrived at the huts, the wolves were hunting around for a snack in the form of the Rabbinels that had just been released by Queen Solinara and her brother, Hotenfaran, from their workshop where they were preparing more food to take care of the growing population of wolves.

"What are they doing?" Navaeha asked as she watched in awe as the wolves hunted down their prey.

"They are going after their lunch. These creatures are called Rabbinels. They were created by my talented wife and her brother to keep the wolves in good shape by giving them something to hunt. Solinara has also infused some much-needed vitamins to help the wolves stay healthy and strong."

"Really? That is unbelievable. She must be quite talented to come up with these animals. I never saw anything like them," Navaeha expressed her surprise.

"They are really strange-looking creatures, King," Aharona added.

"Yes, I guess they are. We are used to seeing them. They are a combination of rabbits and squirrels and are quite sure-footed to give the wolves some exercise."

"Okay, I can see that now. Where are all the rabbits and squirrels?" Aharona looked around searching for some other creatures.

"They are all depleted by the wolves since they came here. That is why Solinara created these creatures to take their place. They procreate fast to keep up with the demand of the wolves' diet."

"I can't believe how large these wolves are. I've never seen anything this large. I don't think we have any on our island with the dragons. The dragons would eat them all anyway."

"That is quite possible," Gateskin agreed.

"I think we are getting a little away from the reason why you summoned us here, King Gateskin," Aharona reminded.

"Yes, I guess we did. Let's go to my conference room where I can explain more to you about our situation with the Catlings."

As the three headed toward the King's house, his queen came out of her workshop with her brother and noticed the sisters. Her face wore an expression of surprise and disapproval which would have warned Gateskin that she was anything but pleased with the sisters' return.

CHAPTER SIXTEEN

The dragons were getting antsy and moved around the area where they had slept. They sniffed the air and smelled something that was vaguely familiar to them.

Evander turned to Callum and hissed in dragon language. "Do you smell that delicious scent in the air?"

Callum sniffed the air bringing a few bushes closer to his nose with the power of his breath. "Hmm, I do smell something familiar. Is it, can it be – wolf?"

"Yes, I think it is. Should we go hunting, my friend?" Evander asked in his sly way.

"No, absolutely not! What would our mistresses say about this? They would have our heads and tails for sure!" Callum exclaimed with an unsteady hiss.

"Are you afraid of Aharona?"

"Not at all, but I do respect and love her. Don't you respect and love Navaeha?"

"Yes, of course I do. But when hunger calls to me I must satisfy it or I will eat her."

"No, you wouldn't, you devil. I know how much you adore her. You would never harm a hair on her head."

"Quite right you are, Callum. But I am getting a little bored and hungry too. Aren't you?"

"Well, maybe a little bored but not quite ravenous yet. Don't you remember that our mistresses said they would always bring us something tasty to eat if we behaved ourselves. Also, King Gateskin brought us a remarkably tasty creature out of thin air. If we play along with them, we will get some more of that."

"Okay, maybe you are correct about that, Callum. But when are they going to return? It has been hours."

"I don't think it has been more than one hour, Evander. You dare to exaggerate again," Callum huffed in exasperation.

"Maybe a little bit, but it does seem like it's been longer, don't you agree? What are we supposed to do to keep ourselves occupied?" Evander snickered.

"Well, we could always go closer to the forest where we were last time. That's where we saw the cat-like creatures. What did they call them?"

"I think I heard the King said they were Catlings, Evander. I do have a better memory than you."

"I think there were plenty of them there. I wonder why there aren't any around here?"

"They would surely eat all the wolves, maybe that's why. There must be a spell on the borders around the village here, Evander"

"Yes, I think that is the reason. Do you think that is why they enlisted the help of our mistresses to come back here?"

"Well, that is quite possible. We should wait to find out what they are planning. Let's wait a little longer to hear about what transpired in their meeting with the King. He must have plans for us to help too," Callum responded.

"I bet they do have plans for us. We are formidable, after all." Evander smiled, sticking out his long tongue to taste the air.

"I can see you are liking the scent too much, Evander. Better stop salivating, you are soaking the ground around us."

"Fine. It's all your fault, Callum. You keep talking about food. That always makes me hungrier. I keep thinking about what the King will bring us when they return. It was the best snack I have ever had."

"I know. I agree, Evander. But we must wait a little longer and then I plan to go closer to the border to see if I can get past the spell that is there and grab a couple of those Catlings for a snack. I don't think the King would miss a couple of them. They will hold us off until King Gateskin brings us another snack. Do you agree?"

"Maybe. But let's wait a little while before we move from here. We never know if there are other people around that will spot us and run in terror. They may try to kill us and then we will be forced to kill them to protect ourselves. That I don't want to do. What would our mistresses say to us then?"

"Nothing good, that's for sure. They may punish us and lock us up for a long time. I don't like that at all," Evander stated anxiously.

The dragons lay down again and soon fell asleep unbeknownst to others around them who were aware of their presence.

CHAPTER SEVENTEEN

Passing by the dragons were two peddlers who were headed to Votovia to sell their wares. They spotted the large creatures who were in deep slumber without their protective camouflage.

"Look, there are two dragons over there! Where did they come from?" one peddler announced in a whisper.

"It can't be? How did they get here? We don't have any dragons in Noella Province. They are all gone to other lands. They were driven away by some Wizards a long time ago."

"But it looks like they have come back. We must spread the word and warn everyone about this! They are dangerous and can destroy our lands."

"Let's get away from here before they spot us and we become their lunch."

The two peddlers tiptoed away from the dragons and hurried on their way to Votovia to report this to King Cavelan.

Soon after King Cavelan was told of these dragons, he contacted King Gateskin to warn him.

Gateskin was sitting at his conference table when he felt a vibration. It was someone trying to reach him through his Channel Spell.

He excused himself from the sisters and opened the Channel Spell. There in front of him was King Cavelan looking quite upset.

"Cavelan, good to see you, or is it? You look disturbed about something, my friend. What is it?"

Cavelan explained what the peddlers had said to him about the dragons. "Do you believe that they have come back here? What are we going to do?"

"No, please let me explain. I hadn't planned on frightening anyone about this but we do have a problem and I was trying to work it out without bothering any of you." He continued to explain about the dangers the Catlings were causing to his wolves.

"I see. But you did not explain where the dragons came from, Gateskin. Do we have some in our province now?"

"No, we do not. Let me introduce you to the mistresses of these two formidable creatures. This is Aharona and her sister, Navaeha. They come from the Island of Dragons called Dragonaria. They came to visit me in the past and I called on them this time to return to assist me in stopping the Catlings from harming our packs of wolves."

"Oh, I understand now. What can I do to help?"

"First of all, please let your people know that they are not in any kind of danger. These dragons are well trained and will not harm any of them. They obey their mistresses and will do only what they tell them to do."

Gateskin looked at Aharona and Navaeha who nodded in agreement.

"Yes, we will make sure they obey us, King Gateskin. Do not worry about them," Aharona stated firmly.

"Ahh, I feel better now, Gateskin. Nice to meet you both," King Cavelan said as he nodded to the women.

The sisters bowed to King Cavelan and smiled. "It is our pleasure to serve Noella Province in any way we can," they responded in unison.

"I would like to meet these creatures sometime but in Sovorotskina. I don't think my people in Votovia would be receptive to them. It might frighten them too much. They have never seen a dragon before, but have heard fierce stories about them."

"That is how most people react to them since they do not know their kind nature. I assure you that they are kind and caring creatures. We have brought them up that way. There are those who do not treat their dragons with kindness thereby teaching them to be aggressive." Aharona explained.

"Hmm, I see," King Cavelan responded. "Many years before we came here dragons flew over our lands and ate all the animals that lived here. Once all the animals were gone, they went after people. That is when a Wizard drove them out of here. They have never returned, that is, until now."

"Don't worry, King Cavelan, we will not be staying here. We are expected home soon, once our father realizes that we left," Navaeha giggled as she looked at her sister who rolled her eyes.

Gateskin cleared his throat and asked, "Are you ready to hear what I propose, ladies?"

"Oh, yes, of course, King Gateskin. Sorry, we got carried away from the subject," Aharona poked her sister to listen and keep quiet.

Gateskin explained, "I need for you to take your dragons into the forest of the Unknown Territory and cull out the Catlings. I am sure Callum and Evander are probably ready for a snack or two by now."

Navaeha's eyes grew wide as she exclaimed, "I don't know if that is a good idea, King."

"Do you think they would not like the taste of these Catlings?"

"No, not at all. I'm sure they will love them, maybe too much and want to keep coming back for more," Navaeha replied.

"I'm sure you can explain to them that this is a one-time thing. I want to cull out the herd and make sure they do not come through the boundaries and attack our people and animals."

Aharona stood and nodded. "Yes, I think we can do that for you, King Gateskin. It would be our pleasure. Do you want to come to watch or should we come back here to report what transpired?"

"I will come with you. I do not have to go into the Unknown Territory to see what you will be doing. I can stand a safe distance away with my excellent vision and see all," Gateskin said with a smile.

King Cavelan excused himself, "I will be going on my way, Gateskin. Best of luck solving this problem. If you need me, just call. But I would be interested to know how it all went just the same. Look forward to your call, my friend."

"That I will do, Cavelan. Talk to you soon."

Turning to the sisters Gateskin said, "I will lead the way and show you how to get through the boundaries."

CHAPTER EIGHTEEN

The sisters joined up with their dragons who were sleeping and just needed a nudge to wake them.

Callum yawned and stretched his long body as his scales glistened in the light that filtered through the trees. Evander did the same and stuck his tongue out again to taste the wolves' scents.

The sisters whispered in the ears of their chargers and explained what they were going to do to help King Gateskin clear out the excessive Catlings.

Callum chuckled in a throaty way as he winked at Gateskin and poked Evander to move along to get their snacks. He knew that King Gateskin would have something tasty for them if they did a commendable job.

The sisters jumped on the backs of the dragons and in a flash, they were up in the air and heading over to the Unknown Territory. They listened to the explanation from the King as they waited for his okay to pass through the boundaries.

As soon as the dragons were in the Unknown Territory and hovering over a copse, they could hear the growling of the Catlings who were close to the borders and milling around trying to find a way through.

"Wow, look at how many there are. How are we going to separate them to allow our dragons to grab one at a time?" Navaeha asked with a wrinkled brow.

"Let's dip down a little closer. They will scatter when they see us and then Callum and Evander can have their pick of one to eat," Aharona stated as she whispered in Callum's ear what to do. Navaeha did the same to Evander.

As soon as the Catlings heard the wings of the dragons coming closer to them, they quickly scattered and ran for their lives. The slower ones were the first ones that the dragons grabbed and gobbled down.

Callum laughed out loud in a guttural way as he licked his teeth clean and dropped down again to grab another Catling. Evander was busy doing the same thing.

After the dragons had each eaten four, they stopped to rest and burped until they were ready to eat again.

Navaeha gagged after seeing the flesh flying around below them that escaped Evander's mouth. She watched in horror as the other Catlings raced over to grab the pieces and eat their fill.

"This is so disgusting, Aharona. I don't think I can stand much more. The smell is horrendous and my stomach is nauseated. I think I am going to be sick if we keep doing this."

"I think we need to let the dragons eat at least six a piece. There are still too many roaming around," Aharona stated.

"What if they injure a few and let the Catlings eat them. That should keep them full so that they won't try to breach the borders," Navaeha clarified.

"That would work if you really don't want to continue. Let me call out to King Gateskin to see if he agrees with this."

King Gateskin was listening and called out to their minds, "That would be fine. Injure as many as you can and then come back here. That should keep them well fed and away from our borders for now."

Aharona responded back to the King and then instructed Evander what to do. He ate one or two more just to satisfy his hunger and then clawed a few as he passed over the herd and flew back to the King.

Callum watched what Evander had done and ate four more to best him before injuring several as he passed by the Catlings who did not know what was happening and were racing back and forth in confusion.

The dragons' mouths were dripping with blood as fur and guts dropped out as they settled down to rest. They were both soon asleep after their large meal.

Aharona apologized for the mess but promised that once the dragons woke up again, they would make sure Callum and Evander cleaned it up.

"I appreciate that, ladies. I don't want any of the villagers to happen upon this mess and think there was carnage."

"I can understand that, King. It does look that way. I think our dragons did a commendable job clearing out some of the Catlings so that they will not be a problem to you for a while," Aharona replied.

"Thank you both. I didn't know what I was going to do if you hadn't come to my rescue. I appreciate the time you took to do this. I hope you will not get into trouble with your father."

"Well, we don't know about that. He doesn't know that we left. We were supposed to stay put until otherwise given permission to travel. He found out about our late journey but doesn't know where we went and we didn't share that either," Navaeha retorted.

"I'm sorry you got into trouble but am relieved that you did not share where you had gone. Maybe you better wake your dragons and be on your way. I can put a spell on you again so that you will not be visible to anyone here until you are safely home," Gateskin explained.

"That would be helpful, King. Thank you," Aharona countered.

The dragons were now snoring loudly with no chance of waking anytime soon. The sisters sighed and sat down to wait.

"Can I offer you some refreshments while you wait for them to wake?" Gateskin asked.

"That would be nice," Navaeha said as she met her sister's eye of displeasure.

"We are fine, King. Our stomachs are a little queasy from watching our dragons devour the Catlings. It was quite unpleasant," Aharona said as she gave her sister a stern look.

"Well, if you change your mind, please let me know. I am only a short distance away. I will be checking the borders to ensure that the Catlings are not still trying to get through. Thank you again."

"Our pleasure, King Gateskin. If you ever need us for anything at all, we are at your disposal."

***

Back at Gateskin's home the children were whispering to each other. "Father is up to something. I can feel it. Where did he go?" Simon asked.

"I know what he is doing," Catalina responded.

"What is he doing?" Simon snapped.

"I thought you knew everything, Simon. Can't you see things?" Catalina asked with a sly smile.

"Never mind. I will figure it out myself. See you later."

"Where are you going, Simon?" Catalina asked with concern.

"I don't know yet. I am trying to feel the air to figure it out." Simon huffed and walked away.

Serena listened to her siblings argue as usual and stepped in to intercede as Simon walked away. She called out, "Wait a minute, Simon. I feel danger close. Do not go out there. Something is happening in the Unknown Territory. We must ask Father about it. Where is he?"

"What? I don't feel anything, Serena. What's wrong?"

Before Serena could answer him, their father stepped out of the woods and came over to the house where they met him at the door.

"Where were you, Father?" Serena asked as she observed his serious face.

"I was working on a problem we have with the Catlings. No worries, everyone. It is all taken care of. We don't have to be concerned about them for a while."

"What did you do, Father?" Simon asked, his curiosity piqued.

"I found a way to keep them from entering the borders."

"How did you do that, Father?" Serena entered the conversation.

"No concern, children. I need to speak with your mother now. Stay away from the borders for today. I don't want any incidents. Okay?"

"Incidents? What does that mean, Father?" Catalina queried.

Gateskin passed by them without further explanation and went to seek his wife to let her know what had transpired.

"I don't think Mother is in a good mood, Father. Watch out," warned Serena.

CHAPTER NINETEEN

Solinara was in the family room straightening out a room that was already clean. She always cleaned when she was upset about something. She was concerned that the sisters had returned without any explanation from her husband. All she could say was that he better have a good one.

Gateskin stopped in his tracks when he spotted his wife cleaning the already spotless room. He knew he was in trouble and better begin explaining and fast. She must have seen the sisters return.

"Hello, dear. What are you doing?" He came up behind her and gave her a hug or at least tried to as she turned around with a scowl on her lovely face.

"What is wrong, Solinara? Why are you looking disgruntled?"

"Really, Gateskin? You didn't see me come out of the workshop with Hotenfaran? I saw the sisters walk away with you. What are they doing here again?"

"Well, I asked them to come. They did not come on their own, I assure you.

They wouldn't do that. They know how you feel about them."

Solinara humphed and turned away from Gateskin.

"Please listen to me, Solinara. I came in to tell you about this."

"All right. Explain yourself."

"Okay. Well, remember I was concerned about the Catlings trying to get through the borders? Well, they nearly grabbed a couple of the wolf cubs who ventured close to the border. I rescued the cubs in time."

"That's good to know. What does this have to do with the sisters?"

"I asked them to come help me cull out the herd of the Catlings. The Catlings have procreated excessively and are out of food. They have decimated the area of all other animals and now are trying to come into our land and eat their way through it."

"Oh no, that can't happen. I remember now you were talking about that. Sorry, I forgot. But how did the sisters help you?"

"Well, they have dragons. The dragons are hungry creatures and will eat any kind of meat. I don't know if you remember about the tales that we heard of the dragons that used to roam the Unknown Territory. They ate their way through just like the Catlings are doing now. They had to be driven away by a Wizard at that time to save the people who lived here. If the Wizard hadn't done that this place would be ruled by dragons now."

"Ah, yes. I do remember. What a thought! We wouldn't be here. The same thing could happen with the Catlings!"

"Exactly, dear. That is why I had to act quickly without first telling you about this."

"Did it work? Did the dragons eat the Catlings?"

"Yes, it did work. They ate a dozen or so Catlings and injured many more to give the surviving Catlings some food source for the time being. We may have to do this again but not right away."

"Does that mean you will call upon the sisters to come again?"

"If I must. There is no other way to control them. I can't just put a spell on them. It would wear off and I would have to keep doing this. I cannot control their hunger."

"What if I supplied some food for them to curb their hunger and make them not want to eat anything but the food I provide?"

"Hmm, that sounds interesting. Can you do that, Solinara? I know how brilliant you are." Gateskin was feeling better now that his wife was no longer angry with him and was taking an active part in solving this problem.

"I will call Hotenfaran and we will begin working on it. I'm sure we can come up with something to keep them at bay."

"That would be wonderful, dear. Okay, I will check on the animals to make sure they are all safe and recheck the borders."

"Wait a minute, Gateskin. Did the sisters leave?"

"Umm, not yet. The dragons are sleeping off all the Catlings they ate. They will leave as soon as the dragons awaken. I will put a spell on them to keep them invisible to all of Noella Province."

"Well, okay. Make sure they do leave."

"I understand you are still upset with them. But they have been polite and respectful since the first time you met them. I wouldn't have them come back if they didn't show respect."

"Really?"

"Yes, really. I didn't like what they said or how they acted the first time either but they have apologized several times over to me and to you. You must forgive and forget, Solinara."

"I will work on it. Besides, I do not like having young, beautiful women hanging on your every word. They are quite smitten with you, you know."

"Are they?" Gateskin smirked.

"Gateskin, you are impossible! I've got work to do. I will make dinner as soon as I can after getting a start on this food with Hotenfaran."

Gateskin bent down to kiss his wife softly on her lips and picked up a blonde curl that was in her face and placed it behind her ear.

She smiled at him and kissed him back before heading over to the workshop and calling out to her brother's mind to meet her there.

Hotenfaran appeared momentarily at the door of the shop and nodded to his sister who still wore a smile on her face after kissing her husband.

"Everything okay, sis?"

"Yes, everything is fine now. We have work to do, brother." She explained to him what they were going to create.

CHAPTER TWENTY

The dragons woke with a start and looked around. It was getting dark now and they couldn't see their mistresses.

Callum stretched and pulled his wings out to feel the air around him. He sniffed the air and burped once and then again.

Evander was still groggy but roused himself and looked at Callum. "What's wrong?"

"I don't see our mistresses. We must have fallen asleep after our big meal. It was delicious but quite filling."

"Yes, Callum, I agree. It was tasty though but too much fat. I think I want something leaner next time. They were large Catlings and heavy to pick up and then chew and swallow. Where are our mistresses?"

"That's what I just said, Evander. I am worried. I don't smell them near us and can't hear them either. Where did they go? I hope they didn't go too close to the borders."

"No, I don't think they would do that, Callum. Give them some credit. They are too smart to do something stupid like that. They know how dangerous these Catlings are."

"So, where are they then?" Callum asked with concern.

"I'm sure they went to the King's house to eat something. They must be hungry since we have been here all day. It's getting dark now. We must have slept a long time."

"I guess we did. Maybe it is the fatty meat we ate. You are right there. We need to cut back on fats, Evander."

"Maybe we should venture closer to the King's house to find them. We should be getting back before their father sees we are gone. He will punish us too, not just them."

"I fear that too, Evander. What should we do?"

"Would the Queen be upset if we came too close to their house and children?"

"Yes, she might. She may think we are there to eat the wolves."

Evander raised his eyebrows and winked at Callum in anticipation.

"Don't even think about that, Evander. I know you. You are insatiable and can eat like there is no tomorrow."

"Don't exaggerate, Callum. I have a delicate stomach. It is so full that I can't fit anything else in there. Well, maybe one small wolf." He leaned down and gobbled up the bits of Catlings that they had left behind until not a smidgeon was left.

"Stop it, right now, Evander! You will get us in trouble. Let's find our mistresses and get out of here before someone spots us and tries to kill us."

"Would they do that?"

"Of course, they would. We are feared creatures. Some of our ancestors once lived here and were driven away."

"How did you know that, Callum? I never heard that before. Who told you?"

"My grandmother told me when I was quite young. She said never to go back here or they would kill us for sure."

"Well, we better hurry up and find our mistresses and get out of here," Evander said as he looked around to make sure no one was there.

"What should we do then?"

"Let's find the King and ask him. He must know where they are. Then we can be on our way."

"All right, let's go but be careful and move stealthily and keep your wings folded close to your body," Callum instructed.

"I'll do my best, Callum. I have larger wings than you do, you know." Evander chuckled.

"But I am more beautiful!" Callum retorted.

Evander hissed and growled as he led the way to find their mistresses.

***

Aharona and Navaeha roamed closer to the borders of the Unknown Territory to try to peek through. They pushed aside some small shrubs and leaned in closer but still couldn't see anything.

Two large Catlings were looking back at them and snarling, their jaws working in tandem as they salivated with the taste of these two bodies that were so close but not yet reachable.

Navaeha leaned still closer until she spotted two sets of glowing eyes looking back at her. She screamed and jumped back but not before one Catling had scratched her arm deep enough to cause it to bleed heavily.

A short distance away the two dragons heard Navaeha's cry and raced up into the sky to find her. They looked through the heavy copse along the borders and spotted two large Catlings who were growling, one licking the blood off his claws.

Navaeha moved away from the border as far as she could and sat down next to her sister who looked over her injured arm. Aharona grabbed a couple of leaves and wiped away the blood so she could see how serious the injury was. She felt like reprimanding her sister for her foolishness in getting too close but knew that this was not the time to do that. Her sister was in pain and needed her to help, not scold her.

Before Aharona could find some medicinal leaves to administer to her sister's arm, she spotted the dragons flying above them and heading their way.

"Oh my god, Navaeha! Our dragons must have heard you scream and are coming to your rescue. We are in deep trouble now. Someone was sure to have spotted them flying overhead."

"Maybe no one was about. We can only hope, Aharona. Let's talk to them to calm them down. They will want to kill more Catlings when they see what one did to me."

"You're right, Navaeha. But it is a good thing that they came to help. They may be able to stop any infection by fire."

"Oh no, not fire, Aharona! What, are you kidding me? That will hurt me more than my arm does now."

"We can't take a chance that you will get an infection from those vile creatures. After all, our dragons ate a dozen of them and have already built up an immunity that they could pass on to you."

"Well, maybe that is possible. But let me see if Evander can use his tongue to wipe away the blood. It would be like an antibiotic, right?"

"I don't know about that. Let me see how it looks." Aharona tried to look at her sister's arm in the dark but couldn't see anything. She beckoned the dragons over and spoke to them.

"Bring some light this way so that I can examine Navaeha's arm. She injured it by putting it into the Unknown Territory. Something scratched her. She may have an infection. Can you help?"

"We know what scratched her, Aharona. We saw the two Catlings licking her blood. Don't worry about them. We ate them."

"Please help us. Let's not worry about the Catlings now," Aharona pleaded.

Evander's eyes glowed giving off a light that centered over Navaeha's arm. It was already swelling and looking discolored. Evander shook his head and reached out his tongue to clean the arm off and turned to Callum.

The two dragons leaned their heads together and conversed and then came back to the sisters and said, "We will have to burn it, Navaeha. It will hurt but I will blow cool air on it right after Evander burns it to kill the infection and close the cuts."

Navaeha sighed but nodded and took a deep breath.

CHAPTER TWENTY-ONE

Gateskin was putting the animals back into their sheds for the night when he heard a scream. He looked around in confusion and called out to his children, "Serena, Simon, Catalina? Where are you?"

Serena was checking on the wolves and their cubs when she heard her father's call. She rushed over to see him as he came out of the animals' shelter.

"What's wrong, Father?"

"Are you all right? Where are your brother and sister?"

"They went back into the house. I told them I would check on the wolves first. Mother called us to come in."

"Did you hear a scream?" Gateskin continued to look around and use his excellent vision to scan the borders around his home.

"No, father. I didn't hear anything. What was it?"

"I don't know, but it sounded like a woman's cry. It frightened me because I thought it was one of you."

"What are you going to do?"

"Go into the house and tell your mother that I will be there as soon as I check this out. It could be a villager in danger. Maybe one of the Catlings got through the borders after all."

"Do you want me to come with you?"

"No, it may be too dangerous for you. Please tell your mother about this and not to worry that I will return soon."

"Yes, Father." Serena watched her father go off into the night and worried just the same as her mother would, but went inside quickly to alert her mother.

After Serena relayed her father's message, Solinara stood by the window looking out for any sign of Gateskin. She sent messages to him, "Where are you, Gateskin? Have you found someone injured?"

"Not yet. But I can see some light up ahead. Don't worry, dear. I will check it out and return shortly. I'm sure it is nothing for you to concern yourself with. Just keep the children inside until I can tell you more."

"Of course. I will keep in touch with you. Let me know if you need me."

"Yes, dear."

The dragons were in the process of heating Navaeha's arm and blowing cool air on it to take away the pain. Navaeha tried to keep her cries as soft as she could but it was intense pain and only stopped after the cool air hit it but would intensify again without the cool air.

Callum blew as much cool air as he could to keep Navaeha comfortable once Evander finished sealing the wound. The two dragons flew up above Navaeha and added more wind by sweeping their wings up and down around her arm.

They were all unaware of Gateskin who stood a short distance away watching them.

"What happened here?" Gateskin called out to them.

Aharona turned around in surprise when she spotted King Gateskin. "Oh, I hope we didn't disturb you and your family. We tried to be quiet but Navaeha has an injury that our dragons are attending to."

"Injury? How did she get injured? I thought you were gone already. I put a spell on the air above that would have covered you and kept you safe all the way home. I'm sure it is gone now."

Navaeha was in too much discomfort to answer so Aharona responded, "My sister was injured when a Catling reached through the boundary and scratched her arm. It appeared to be getting infected so our dragons came to the rescue and burned and sealed the cuts. She is in a lot of pain even with all the cool air being blown over it."

King Gateskin came closer to look. He raised his hands over Navaeha's arm and brought up a light to inspect it. "It looks red but is perfectly sealed and not bleeding now. I'm sure you are in pain. Solinara can put a salve on it to stop the pain. Come with me, all of you, dragons included."

Aharona started to refuse, "No, we cannot do that! Solinara will be quite upset. We were supposed to be gone by now."

"I know, but you are still here and this must be taken care of right away. You cannot go home like this. Follow me. Keep your dragons close and don't let them fly. I will put a spell around us to keep them invisible."

The sisters nodded and explained this to their dragons who agreed and kept pace with the King keeping their wings close to their bodies.

Solinara sent another message to Gateskin for an update. He quickly but reluctantly replied, "I am heading back now. I have an injury that needs your salve. We will be there shortly."

Gateskin hoped Solinara would be pleasant to these unwelcome visitors and not too shocked over the dragons.

The children were at the windows watching their father with two figures and something that was under cover of a spell. They couldn't make out what it was but opened the door and peered out for a closer look.

Solinara opened the door wider to welcome in her husband but then stepped back when she saw the sisters and two huge creatures behind them, due to her ability to see through the shield that covered them.

CHAPTER TWENTY-TWO

Solinara cried out, "What are they doing here? I thought they would be gone by now after killing the Catlings. These creatures cannot come into my home."

The sisters turned around to leave but were stopped by Gateskin who guided them back toward the door. "She does not mean you. Solinara means the dragons. They are too big to fit inside. They will have to stay here under my spell. They will not go near the wolves for any reason or else I will have to put another spell on them."

Gateskin waited for the sisters to explain to the dragons what he said. The dragons nodded in his direction and lay down to take a nap.

The children's eyes were wide with delight and hurried to get near the sleeping creatures.

"Where do you three think you are going?" Gateskin exclaimed.

Serena begged, "Father, we want to go see the dragons. They are so beautiful! We've never seen a dragon before; well not this close I mean. We want to get a good look at them again."

Simon leaned closer but was stopped by his father's arm. "Please, Father, let us see them just this once up close."

Catalina smiled at her father and batted her eyes. This always got her way, but not this time. "Oh, Father, please. They are like rainbows – so colorful. I've never seen anything so magnificent before!"

"Magnificent? That is a big word for you, little one." Gateskin was weakening as he looked at his children's unhappy faces.

"All right, just a quick peek. Let me go with you. I don't want them to eat one of you for a snack even though they are quite full, I'm sure, from all the Catlings they gobbled."

"Catlings? They ate Catlings, Father?" Catalina gasped.

"Oh, umm, yes. I didn't mean to share that with you. Sorry about that."

Serena giggled and said, "That's okay, Father. We figured you were going to find a way to keep the Catlings away from the borders. Eating some of them may have helped. Right?"

"Yes, I think it did for now. We may have to do this again or come up with another way to cull the herd. Your mother is working on something that may help."

Solinara was attending to Navaeha's arm while she kept a close watch on the children as they looked at the dragons.

"Are my children safe that close to those creatures?" Solinara asked the sisters in a gruff voice.

"Of course, Queen Solinara. Callum and Evander will never hurt children," Aharona responded in a soft voice.

"Make sure they do not," Solinara added, with a stern look.

"Please, Queen, we are sorry about the last time we were here. Do you think we can be friends? We do not want to harm any of your family and only want to come in peace and friendship," Aharona said with a tentative smile.

"I…okay. But I will be keeping my eye on both of you and want to make sure you treat my husband with respect, not like before."

"Of course, we respect King Gateskin and hold him with the utmost affinity."

"Thank you, Aharona. Now, Navaeha, how is your arm feeling?"

Navaeha smiled for the first time since this happened. "It is amazing! I don't feel any pain even though it is still a little red but healing quicker now. What did you do, Queen?"

"This is a special salve that I use for pain. I always used it on my children when they fell, had scrapes, burns and even for their sore mouths when they were teething. It works wonders and helps to heal fully."

"Yes, I can see that! I can't thank you enough, Queen Solinara, for helping me. I know we are not your favorite visitors. We plan to leave now that I am healing. I don't think there will be any scar for my father to see either."

"That is correct. There will not be a scar, for this salve heals from the inside out, and once it has completed its magic, you will never know you had any cuts there."

"Thank you!!" Navaeha sighed happily.

"By the way, how did you get these cuts?"

Navaeha explained about her mishap with the Catlings. "I know it was not a smart thing to do, Queen. But I guess I learned my lesson now. I will never get that close to the borders again."

"That is good to know. It could have been worse. You could have been killed and then..."

"I know. I shudder to think of what could have happened to my sister," Aharona exhaled. "We appreciate your kindness, Queen, and can't thank you enough!" Aharona and Navaeha bowed down to Solinara and stayed down until she tapped them on their heads to get up.

"That is not necessary, ladies. I would have done this for anyone in need. I think we can be friends but promise me to keep those dragons close to you and away from our children, shed animals and wolves."

"Of course. We will always do that. But now I think it is time for us to take our leave. We have overstayed our visit and our father will be looking for us since it's time for dinner."

"Right! Hopefully he has been too busy to realize we are not there, Navaeha. We may be punished for the next month if he finds that we disobeyed him again."

Solinara shook the girls' outstretched hands and followed them out to the yard where her family was talking to the dragons. Solinara handed a bag of tea leaves to the sisters to take back home to their mother.

Aharona bowed again to the Queen and thanked her for the tea saying, "This may work as a peace offering to our mother. I'm sure she will love it. Thank you."

"You are most welcome. I hope she does love it."

The sisters watched in awe as the King's children were enjoying their dragons.

The children were enthralled with them. Serena found that she could converse with the dragons in her head much to the chagrin of her sister and brother who frowned in disapproval.

The dragons were having a good time with the children and being very careful not to injure them as the children took turns sitting on Callum's and Evander's backs.

A fluttering suddenly could be heard above them and everyone looked up.

CHAPTER TWENTY-THREE

Spindle flew down from the tree nearby and settled next to Serena with a sigh. "How are you, Serena? What do we have here? Dragons, they are back again? Are they staying for a while?"

"I'm fine, Spindle. They are our visitors but will be leaving soon. Let me introduce you to them. The last time you saw them you did not get to know them by name. This one with the iridescent and colorful rainbow body and huge green eyes is Callum. This is Evander with the larger wings, sparkling blue eyes and blue, red, and gold-glowing scales. They are both so beautiful, don't you think so?" Serena petted each one and smiled at them as she heard their thoughts in her mind.

"Nice to officially meet you both, Callum, and Evander. Don't tell me you can hear their thoughts, Serena? That is amazing!"

Serena giggled and nodded to the dragons and turned to Spindle to share what they had said to her about him. "Yes, I can. They think you are quite a comical creature and something they have never seen before. They want you to come closer so they can see you better."

"What? Are they going to eat me?" Spindle's voice trembled.

"No, silly. They don't eat wood. They just want to look at you. They find you as interesting as you do them. Go ahead, don't be afraid."

"Afraid! I am not afraid of anything or anyone," Spindle declared in a firm tone.

"I knew that, Spindle. Go ahead." Serena gave Spindle a little push.

Callum sniffed Spindle from head to toe and then licked his face, much to the surprise of the Sprite.

Evander did the same and then whispered in Spindle's ear, "Don't worry about him. He is not scary at all. But me – that's different!" Evander chuckled when he saw the shock on the

Sprite's face which changed from brown to green when he was upset or embarrassed.

"Are you okay, Spindle?" Serena rushed to his side.

"I'm fine. I think Evander was trying to intimidate me. But I don't intimidate easily, dragon." He stared at Evander and met his glowing blue eyes with his own brown-eyed glare.

Evander stepped forward and apologized to Spindle, "Sorry about that, little guy. I didn't mean anything by that. I find you quite amazing! Can we be friends now?"

Spindle reached out his little brown hand and shook the offered claws of the dragon who bowed down and then looked up with a nod and smile.

Callum chuckled, "My friend here can be a bully at times. Don't pay attention to him. I, on the other hand, will promise to be your friend always, Spindle."

"Thank you both. By the way, where do you come from and why did you return?"

Serena answered for them, "They come from Dragonaria, the Land of Dragons. They were summoned by my father to help with the Catlings' invasion."

"Catlings' invasion? I knew they were procreating quickly but did they invade Sovorotskina? I did not see any around here and I have been keeping watch."

King Gateskin joined in the conversation, "I requested their help to cull the herd of Catlings who nearly ate a couple of our wolf cubs recently."

"Oh no. That is not surprising, though. They must be out of food in the Unknown Territory if there are so many of them."

"Exactly, Spindle. The owners, two sisters, who are heading this way, told the dragons to eat as many of the Catlings as they could to help us and injured a few more."

"Did it work?" Spindle queried.

"Well, for a little while it has helped. I know they will get hungry after eating the ones that the dragons injured for them and come looking this way again."

"What can I do to help you, King?"

"You are here now and will keep an eye on the borders from your trees and let me know if they are getting too close to the borders in great numbers again."

"Right away, King Gateskin. Whatever you need me to do, I will do."

"Thank you, Spindle."

"I'm sorry I have been busy with my father and mother. He hasn't been feeling well and I am taking on some of the chores that he always did."

"I'm sorry to hear that. If there is anything we can do to help you, please call me. Solinara can help with her salves and spells to heal any ailment he may have."

"I was thinking along those lines and told my mother so. She didn't want to bother you. She told me that you looked concerned about something and quite busy rushing around the land. Now I know it was about the Catlings."

"Yes, it was, but we are okay for now. I will come visit your father shortly after my visitors leave to see how he is doing while you check the borders."

"Thank you. He would like that."

"King Gateskin, we are ready to leave now. Solinara has been gracious enough to heal my sister."

"That's good to hear. Let me see that cut, Navaeha."

"Who is this little creature?" Navaeha exclaimed as she extended her arm to the King.

"It is truly better. You did a wonderful job, Solinara. It is almost healed," Gateskin exclaimed as he searched Navaeha's arm for a scar.

"Thank you, dear," Solinara responded.

"Oh, this is Spindle. He is a Sprite and is my Head Guard. Spindle, this is Aharona and Navaeha who are the mistresses of these incredible dragons," Gateskin said.

Spindle bowed to the ladies and extended his hand in greeting. "Nice to meet you, Aharona and Navaeha."

"It is our pleasure, Spindle. You are a Sprite? We have never seen Sprites before. They do not exist on our island.

That could be because we don’t have as many trees as you do here.”

“That could be right. We do need our trees to live in and for protection.”

“Did you meet our dragons?” Navaeha asked.

“Yes, we did meet twice. I think we have become friends now.”

“Now? What happened when you first met? Did Evander give you a hard time?” Navaeha asked as she met her dragon’s eye.

“Everything is fine. No worries. It was nice to meet you all but I need to get to work doing the King’s bidding. Good evening to you.”

Spindle flew away in a flash landing on his tree as he gazed down into the forest of the Unknown Territory.

“Wow, he is quite a remarkable little creature!” Aharona exclaimed.

Serena smiled and said, "Yes, he is," as her face grew blotches of crimson on her cheeks.

The sisters exchanged smiles at this and proceeded to get their dragons ready for takeoff. They knew there would be problems ahead for them once they reached home.

Aharona tucked the tea inside her cloak and patted it for good luck. She knew they would need it.

CHAPTER TWENTY-FOUR

Isla and Marcellus paced back and forth. They had looked all over the island for their daughters. They kept searching the skies but so far there was no sign of their errant daughters.

"I don't believe they did this again, Marcellus. It is so unlike them to be so belligerent."

"Are you speaking of our daughters or someone else's, my dear?" Marcellus remarked in a sharp tone.

"Now, Marcellus, there is no reason for you to use that tone with me. Our girls are adventuresome and love to travel. They do get a little antsy sitting around here with nothing to do."

"Yes, that is true. Maybe it is time for them to take on some more responsibility. I will have to lay the law down and give them plenty to keep them busy and out of trouble. You would think at their ages that they would be more grown up."

Before Isla could respond they heard a rustle in the bushes close to where they were standing by the girls' huts. The dragons suddenly appeared as if they came out of a cloud as they descended onto the ground.

Aharona and Navaeha jumped off their dragons and came to stand in front of their parents who were shaking their heads and frowning.

"Umm, sorry, Father, Mother, we are late getting back. We went for a ride because we were getting restless and so were our dragons. They needed to get some exercise."

Their father waited for more information as he tapped his foot on the ground with arms tightly folded against his chest to keep from raising his hand to his daughters in anger.

Isla touched her husband's arm and whispered into his ear. "Please calm down, Marcellus. Let the girls explain."

"I am waiting. There is more that you are not telling me, Aharona. You are the older one and should be more responsible. What is it that you are not sharing?"

"Sorry, Father. We…umm…we went to the Province of Noella."

"You what?! You are forbidden to go there or anywhere near that land. I told you they do not like dragons in that part of the world. You cannot take a chance that they will kill you and your dragons just for flying by."

"Well, we didn't just fly by, Father," Navaeha added.

"What? You mean you landed there?"

"Yes, Father. We did but only because we were requested to go back by King Gateskin of Sovorotskina." Aharona slapped her sister's hand in warning.

"What do you mean go back?"

"We…we…visited once before."

"Aharona! Are you out of your mind?" her father exclaimed as his face turned beet red.

"Marcellus, calm down. I don't want you to have a heart attack. You need to listen to the girls. I'm sure they had a legitimate reason for going there and then returning," Isla responded firmly.

Navaeha looked at her sister and then closed her mouth as Aharona began to explain, "Father we did not plan on landing there the first time but it looked so beautiful and green. We just had to drop down. Besides, Evander and Callum needed to rest. It was a long trip."

"Did you encounter any trouble when you landed?"

"Not really, Father, but we did see some unusual creatures called Catlings. That is the reason why we had to go back."

"Wait a minute. You did not explain why you were requested to go back. Did you meet King Gateskin?"

The sisters exchanged confused expressions over their father's mention of King Gateskin.

"Yes, that is what I said before, Father. He was the one who requested we return to help him with the Catlings."

"Hmm. What about these Catlings?" her father asked in confusion.

"Well, it seems that the Catlings had nothing left to eat since they had decimated all the other creatures living in the UT or Unknown Territory."

"Unknown Territory?"

"Yes, that is what the area where the Catlings live is called. It is separate from the rest of the province but still part of it by boundaries."

"How can it be separate if it is part of it?"

"Sorry, Father. I will try to explain. King Gateskin is a Wizard and he is quite powerful. He has put a spell or spells on the borders separating his land from the Unknown Territory because of the Catlings. They have been trying to breach the borders to eat some wolves that are in Sovorotskina."

"Wolves?" her father became more confused.

"Yes, they have wolves there too. It is so beautiful, wild and a wonderful place to visit. We were happy to hear from King Gateskin and that he wanted us to go back there."

"How did he contact you?"

"I told you he is a Wizard, one of the most powerful in the whole province. His wife is a fairy and she is quite powerful too. Even their children can do things unheard of here."

"I see. But what could *you* do to help him?"

"We have something that they do not have - dragons!"

"Ah, now I understand. But that land sent the dragons away to settle here on our island. We accepted them as long as they did not harm us."

"Yes, I know all about that, Father. We trained them to obey as you taught us and they have been our friends ever since."

"What you don't understand, girls, is that these people of Noella Province could kill you and your dragons if they so desired since they are so powerful. You cannot go back there again."

"But, Father! They may need us again. We helped them cull the herd of

Catlings and we will need to do that again soon if the creatures continue to procreate."

"That is their problem, not yours or ours. You are forbidden to return there. Do you understand me?"

Aharona and Navaeha exchanged shocked expressions. They even looked at their mother who shook her head and walked away.

"You can't do this, Father," Aharona cried out.

Her father followed close behind their mother and left the sisters standing there without any idea what they were going to do next.

"Aharona, give mother the tea. Maybe that will help."

"Too late. She is gone."

CHAPTER TWENTY-FIVE

Back in Sovorotskina Gateskin went to visit Abason, Spindle's father. He wanted to make sure that the Head Council of the Sprites was doing better. He planned to alert Solinara to get some of her herbs and potions ready to administer them to Abason if needed.

Anabal, Abason's wife, met Gateskin as he came to the base of their tree. "Welcome King Gateskin. I will come down there to speak with you. Abason is not well enough to move from his bed."

"That is why I came as soon as Spindle told me about his father being ill. What can I do to help? Can I send Solinara over with some of her potions and herbs?"

"I don't know what will help him, King. He is getting old and somewhat feeble. He has been pushing himself too much lately with Spindle's new position as your Head Guard. He is taking on more jobs that our son once did for us."

"I am so sorry to hear that. I will relieve Spindle of any extra responsibilities if that will help so he can assist your husband and ease his burdens."

"I don't think that will help now. It may be too late," Anabal cried out as she wiped her eyes and blew her nose on a cloth she held tightly in her hands.

"No, I do not think so, Anabal. I will call Solinara right now to come."

"I appreciate your help, King Gateskin. I do not know what else to do at this point."

"It's okay. Don't worry. We will have your husband up and about in no time," Gateskin replied in a calm and soft tone as he summoned his wife through his thoughts.

No sooner did he finish his summons to Solinara that she appeared next to him and Anabal.

"I have brought my herbs and potions and will mix them right now so you can administer them immediately to Abason. I assure you he will perk up immediately after the first spoonful."

"Thank you, Queen Solinara. I can't tell you enough how much I appreciate your kindness to help us. I didn't want to bother either one of you but I knew that Spindle would tell you."

"We are happy that he did. We will take care of him, Anabal. Everything will be okay," Gateskin said as he patted Anabal on her shoulder as gently as he could because of her small stature.

Solinara put the potion into a small thimble-size bottle and handed it to Anabal who struggled with the small bottle even though it was diminutive.

Solinara reached forward to help Anabal lift the bottle up to the tree. She floated next to the Sprite and then after ensuring Anabel had the bottle securely in hand, Solinara floated back down to Gateskin.

"Thank you, Queen. I will give him some of this right away. I will let you know how he does."

"Yes, please do that. You can always send Spindle over to us with the news. I know it will be good, so don't worry."

Anabal nodded and blew them a kiss as she disappeared into her tree house to take care of her husband.

Solinara smiled and turned to Gateskin. "Do you think Abason will recover?"

"I have no doubt, my dear, of your powers of healing. He will recover fully, don't worry."

"I suppose. But it is strange that he has become sick like this. He has always been so healthy and strong for his advanced age."

"Yes, I agree. But I know that whatever ails him will pass. Look what you have done for everyone you have treated. They always returned to good health. Please don't worry."

"I…okay. I will not worry for now. I will keep an eye and ear out for Spindle with the news, good or bad."

CHAPTER TWENTY-SIX

Spindle was busy watching the borders for any signs of trouble from the Catlings. He had visited fellow Sprites in neighboring trees to tell them to keep watch for any of these creatures who were trying to break the spell and enter Sovorotskina.

He spotted something large coming their way in the sky. He focused on it as it got closer. What was it?

***

King Kaposkaran and Queen Beregina of Parotovina, Land of Darkness and Evil, were arguing about the moss that was still around their land. "Why can't we get rid of this pesky stuff?"

"You should be the one to do that, Beregina. Especially since you put it there with your spell."

"Don't start that again, Kaposkaran! I've had enough of you!" Beregina stormed away before she said anything more.

Kaposkaran shook his head and picked up a piece of the moss and threw it into the fire that was in the square. It wasn't moving or growing anymore but just sitting there. He feared that it might begin to take over his kingdom though in some way if he didn't do something. He had heard that the other kings had found a solution and rid their lands of it. He would have to find out how they did it. He called one of his men to the castle conference room.

"I need you to visit some of the other lands and find out how they got rid of this moss. Don't let them know where you came from or who requested you do this. Do you understand?"

"Yes, King Kaposkaran, I understand perfectly. When do you want me to go?"

"Now, you imbecile. Right now, get moving or I will have your head!"

"Yes sir! Right away, King. I am going." The man whispered to himself; "I will have to tell my wife first." He didn't want the King to hear him say this though or he would have lost his head.

Meanwhile, Beregina sulked in her room and looked for a new spell in her book. "Maybe I can use another spell to get rid of this stuff once and for all. I don't want him to keep insulting me like that. I am a great and powerful fairy. I will come up with a solution without anyone's help."

She became distracted when she spotted a man from her window foraging in the garbage cans.

***

Spindle watched the sky and the large thing that was coming his way. He couldn't believe his eyes. It was a Quintaroon, a creature that was created from a man by King Kaposkaran. "Where did this come from? I thought it was gone for good."

He flew back to his tree to check on his father first and then he would alert Gateskin of this thing right away.

Abason was sitting up in his bed when Spindle arrived. "How are you doing, Father?"

"Feeling a lot better, son. Your friend's mother is a powerful fairy. She gave your mother a potion for me. It was miraculous. I felt as if I was dying before. I didn't want to tell you or your mother that though."

"Thank goodness you are better. Yes, Queen Solinara is powerful indeed. We are fortunate to live here so close to the King and Queen. I owe them more than I can ever repay."

"Me also, my son. Don't worry, I will do all I can to repay them in my own way and in due time."

"I need to leave right away, Father, but I wanted to check on you first. There is a danger coming this way and I need to alert King Gateskin."

"What is it, Spindle?" Abason asked in alarm.

Spindle explained about seeing the Quintaroon.

"I thought it was under King Gateskin's control and not a danger to us anymore."

"Evidently, it escaped and is now here. See you later, Father. I must go."

"Of course, do your duty, son. I will be here if you need me."

Spindle nodded and flew away to the King's home.

CHAPTER TWENTY-SEVEN

After much explanation, Gateskin brought Spindle into his conference room to discuss the problem about the Quintaroon.

"This cannot be the same Quintaroon. I put it in a cabin and it is under a spell not to turn back into this creature. It is now a man again and quite docile," Gateskin explained.

"I thought so, King. But what I saw could be another one. Maybe King Kaposkaran created another one."

"The only way to find out is to open up my Channel Spell and speak with Kaposkaran," Gateskin explained as he waited for the Parotovinan King to answer.

When King Kaposkaran didn't answer, Gateskin opened up a window to check on Quintal who was once a Quintaroon. The man was sleeping on his cot peacefully with no signs of the creature on his face or body.

"That is strange, King. I know what I saw. It was a Quintaroon!" Spindle's voice raised in surprise. “How can that be?”

“I trust your eyes, Spindle. It appears that we have another one. Who knows why Kaposkaran would want to do that now. He has something planned. That is why he is not answering my call.”

“Do you want me to check with my fellow Sprites closer to Parotovina about this? Maybe they know something.”

“Yes, please do that right away, Spindle. I will keep trying Kaposkaran. How is your father?”

“Oh, sorry, I forgot to mention he is sitting up now and talking coherently. He said he is feeling a lot better thanks to the Queen’s administration. He is truly indebted to you both.”

“No problem, Spindle. Don’t even think about that. Go on your way now. I’m happy to hear that Abason is better.”

Spindle bowed to Gateskin as he excused himself to deliver his messages.

Gateskin waited in his conference room for the call he made to Kaposkaran to be picked up. He left it open as he went to find his wife to deliver the good news about Abason.

Back in Parotovina, King Kaposkaran saw the channel opening and ignored it. He would not kowtow to the King of Sovorotskina. Once his man returned, he would have the solution to the moss problem. He could not understand why Gateskin was summoning him now.

Kaposkaran stayed put watching the channel quiver as it waited for his response. After several minutes he couldn't contain his curiosity any longer and answered it.

"What do you want, Gateskin? I am a busy man."

There was no answer. Just an empty conference room. No sign of Gateskin.

"Where did he go?" Kaposkaran was ready to hang up when he saw Gateskin's face fill the window.

"Ah, Kaposkaran, there you are. Did I get you at an inopportune time?" Gateskin snickered.

"No, Gateskin. I was sitting here deciding whether to answer you or not. What is it you want?"

"Well, it appears that there is another Quintaroon on my land. It just arrived."

"What do you mean another Quintaroon? There is only one. I should know because I created it. You have the one that escaped my land. When are you going to release it and let it return to me?"

"What makes you think that I have it here?"

"I know it came there. Because…I s… Never mind!"

"You sent it here to spy on me, didn't you, Kaposkaran?"

"No, I did not. It went on its own. I want it back now!"

"I can't send anything back if I don't have it."

Kaposkaran grumbled in disbelief. "Is that all you want from me, Gateskin?"

"Well, there is something else.

CHAPTER TWENTY-EIGHT

The Parotovinan guard traveled through the borders of the different lands as he questioned people along his way about the moss and how they rid their lands of it.

Several villagers told of a spell that was cast to rid the lands of the moss and how it was created by King Gateskin and his Wizards.

"That is interesting. Can you tell me more about how they did that?"

"No, we aren't Wizards and don't know any magic. Who are you and why are you asking this. Where do you come from?"

The guard moved away from the man after he questioned him and went to the next land to see if he could discover something more.

He wasn't having any luck but persevered and finally moved across the lake and into Sovorotskina. He knew that was probably where he would find his answer. If he didn't find one soon his family could be in danger from the King's ire.

He stayed away from the borders of the Unknown Territory since he knew the dangers that were there with the

Catlings. They were ugly, vile creatures and he did not want to end up being their next meal. He bent down to drink from the stream nearby and nibbled on some greens that were edible. He hadn't had anything to eat all day. As he leaned over, he spotted something lying in the grass. He moved closer to see what it was.

***

Queen Beregina smiled to herself. She had just created something that her husband could never do. She couldn't wait to share this with him. She would show him who had more power in this land. She guffawed as she went to find him.

Kaposkaran was taking a nap in his room and was startled awake by his wife's voice which always grated on his nerves.

"What do you want, Beregina? I thought we weren't speaking."

"Oh, I think you will want to know about this, my dear. I just did something that you have not been able to do with the help of your Wizards."

"What is that? Did you cook something with your own two hands?" he chuckled as he wiped the sleep from his eyes and looked at her.

She pulled him out of bed and told him to follow her to her workshop. "I have something to show you."

"All right. Wait a minute let me get my shoes on. I don't like to walk around the castle without them. The stone is much too cold."

"Well, hurry up."

"I'm coming," Kaposkaran grumbled with impatience.

When they arrived at Beregina's workshop she stopped and stared. It was gone!

"I don't see anything extraordinary here, Beregina. What are you trying to show me, that you cleaned your workshop yourself? It certainly looks like it. It is a mess!" Kaposkaran laughed so hard he nearly fell over.

"Quiet! It was here when I left. Where did it go?"

"What? I don't see anything."

"That's right. It is not here now. I created something that you were unable to do on your own. But now it has escaped. We must find it!"

"What did you do, Beregina? What escaped? Is it dangerous? Did you use the Dark Magic again?" King

Kaposkaran's voice rose an octave as he waited for his wife to answer.

Beregina shook her head and sat down. She didn't answer but her face expressed her fear at what she had done.

"Answer me, Beregina. What did you do now?"

CHAPTER TWENTY-NINE

The sleeping Quintaroon woke when it smelled something tasty - a man. It looked up at the startled man who stood a few feet away from it.

"What are you?" the man asked.

The Quintaroon did not have the ability to speak but reached forward with its long fingers and talons to grip the man in a vise.

"What are you doing? Don't hurt me, please! I am King Kaposkaran's guard. You cannot harm me. He will come after you if you do."

The Quintaroon ignored the screams of the man and kept squeezing him until the man turned red, then blue and dropped to the ground in death. The man's last thoughts were of his family who he would never see again. The creature ate the man and lay down to take another nap now that he was full.

There was nothing left of the man but his clothes that lay in a heap, bloodied, and shredded.

***

A scream ran out through Skina Forest which borders the Unknown Territory. Spindle heard it and passed the word to all the Sprites to check around them for the source.

Spindle quickly received word that it was a villager who was out cutting firewood when he stumbled on some bloody clothes. He knew that the King would want to be informed right away.

The Sprite flew to the King's house once again to put in his report. The other Sprites guided the startled man, who had found the clothes, to King Gateskin's per Spindle's request.

Gateskin was out in the yard tending to the garden and the animals along with his children when he saw Spindle beckoning him over.

"Excuse me, children. I need to speak with Spindle. Pick the vegetables that are ready, and continue feeding and brushing the animals. Check out the hens also, Serena, and bring in the eggs if there are any there. Your mother wants to use them right away."

"Okay, Father," Serena responded as she kept her eyes on Spindle who smiled in return when he spotted her looking at him.

Spindle spoke in a whisper, "I need to share something with you of utmost urgency, King. This man who is coming along behind me needs to share something with you that he discovered."

The man stepped forward and followed behind Spindle and Gateskin into the King's house and along to his conference room.

"What is going on, Spindle? Is your father all right?"

"Oh, he is fine, King. This is something that I think this man will be able to explain. I am still learning the facts about this." Spindle pointed to the man to begin.

The man looked at the Sprite and the King with frightened eyes. "I am Harold, King Gateskin. I am honored to meet you in person. I live at the edge of the village nearest Ailylene Mountain. I was out cutting some wood for my stove. It is getting a little colder at night when I stumbled across some clothes that were covered in blood." Spindle held out the clothes for the King to inspect.

"I saw a trail of blood and guts a short distance away then…" The man stopped when he began to shake all over.

"You are all right now, Harold. Nothing is going to harm you. Please continue," Gateskin pleaded.

"Yes, yes, of course. I am still shaken from this. My heart feels like it will jump out of my chest. It was so horrendous. I am only relieved that I did not bring my children with me as I usually do."

"I understand but you must explain what you saw, Harold," Gateskin implored.

CHAPTER THIRTY

"I followed the trail for a short time and then had to hide behind some bushes because I saw a…a…horrible creature. It was a Quintaroon just like the one that terrorized us once before. I don't think it saw me as I hurried away, but I couldn't keep myself from screaming for help as I ran. I never looked back because I was afraid that it was right behind me and would grab me any minute!" Harold took deep gulps of air and collapsed sideways almost falling out of the chair.

The King caught the man and pushed him back into the chair.

"Spindle, please ask Solinara to get Harold a glass of water and some calming potion right away."

"Yes, King." Spindle flew to the kitchen and around the house but couldn't find Solinara. He got a glass and filled it half-full with water and did his best to carry it back to the man.

"Thank you, Spindle," the man responded as he drained the glass in one gulp and sighed.

"I couldn't find Solinara. She was nowhere in the house."

"That's okay, Spindle. Thank you. I will summon her. I think you need to stay here with Harold until I find her."

"Yes, of course. I will not leave him, King."

Harold sat there and kept shivering as he thought of what he had told them. "I'm sorry for being a bother, Spindle. I can't get the images out of my mind of that creature and all the blood and guts."

"I can imagine it but really don't want to, Harold. I am happy to see that it did not come after you."

"Me too!" Harold tried to smile but shivered instead. "I need to go back home to let my wife know where I am. She will be worried about me being away for so long. My family could be in danger too."

"I will take you back as soon as the King returns with Queen Solinara. She is going to give you something to relax."

"No, I don't need anything. I need to have all my senses to go home and protect my family from this thing out there."

Before Spindle could respond, the King and Queen came into the room. Solinara carried her basket of potions and leaned over to speak to Harold.

"How are you doing, Harold? I have something that will help you relax and forget about what you saw."

"I appreciate your help, Queen Solinara, but I must return home. My family could be in danger. That creature is still out there somewhere."

"Harold, that is not your job to worry about now. I will take care of the Quintaroon. Spindle is going to gather the rest of my men and we will capture it," Gateskin said with urgency.

"Take this and you will feel better soon, Harold," Solinara explained as she handed him a glass with green fluid.

Gateskin spoke to his wife in her head, "Get the children inside and make sure all the animals are safely inside the barn. I don't want anyone or anything injured. Tell Serena to speak with the wolves and inform them of the danger to them and their cubs."

"Of course, dear. Don't worry about anything here. I will take care of the children and animals. You take care of the villagers. They may be in danger if they are out in the woods."

Gateskin nodded to his wife and turned to the trembling man. "I will guide you on your way home, Harold. Come with us now," Gateskin instructed.

Spindle flew ahead to contact the other Sprites for any updates on where the creature was now.

CHAPTER THIRTY-ONE

Spindle gathered all the King's men along with Mitteran, the second Head Guard in command, who assisted Spindle at times like this, in front of his tree house. He informed them of what had transpired and then flew back to hover over Gateskin's shoulder as the King continued to give instructions of what he wanted his men to do.

"Thank you, men, for your quick response. As Spindle mentioned to you, we have another Quintaroon. It appears King Kaposkaran is at it again. I am expecting that his men will be searching for this creature. If you do see them, speak to them without fighting. Explain that you are going to help them find it and bring it back here. You are not to kill it. Keep them from doing the same. I'm sure Kaposkaran does not want it harmed. He must have plans for it."

"Yes, King Gateskin," the men replied and followed Spindle through Skina Forest close to the Unknown Territory as they looked for tracks and signs of the carnage that it may have left behind.

Gateskin quickly returned home to secure the area and send a message to the villagers through their minds. "Be aware that there is danger afoot. A new Quintaroon is about. Keep your children and livestock sheltered safely away until I report that it is safe. I will contact you as soon as my men capture it."

Men and women scurried about their properties to gather the children and livestock. They picked up tools to keep at the ready in case they had to fight it off. They were brave men and women who were not afraid of dealing with the unexpected. They trusted their King to protect them and would always support him in whatever he requested from them.

***

Deep in Skina Forest the creature roamed in search of another meal. It had an insatiable appetite but there was nothing around to satisfy it unless it could find another human. It heard a human scream earlier but the person had run away. The creature was still too full at that time to chase the man. Now it wished that it had.

It sniffed the air and smelled something different. It pushed its way through the copse into another forest as it followed the intriguing scent.

The creature did not know what it was and only knew that it was hungry when it had escaped that woman who chained it in a cell. It could not touch her or it would have eaten her then and there. She had some power over it and told it to stay there until she returned. When she didn't come back right away, it broke out of the cell and ran through the woods. It ran so fast that it found itself flying. It kept flying until it came to the first forest and lay down to take a nap. It had happened upon that first man and ate its fill, but that is all it could remember.

***

Back in Parotovina, Queen Beregina explained to her husband about what she had created by using a pauper she found roaming around the streets.

“You did what? Are you crazy? What man did you use?”

“I don’t know who he was. He was a pauper and digging inside the barrels of garbage for something to eat. He was no better than the garbage he ate.”

“Is it a Quintaroon? We lost one of these already. It went to Sovorotskina and never returned. It was supposed to spy on Gateskin for me. The problem is I cannot get it back because Gateskin knows that I was the one who sent it there. Do you know where this one could have gone?”

"Yes, it is a Quintaroon, but I didn't finish with it. I don't know where it could have gone. I explained to it that it was to stay here until I returned. But it must have gotten hungry and went to find something to eat. We better warn our people about it. It could eat them or their animals."

"Right, it could. What were you thinking, Beregina? No, forget it! You were not thinking!" Kaposkaran marched out of the workshop and back to his conference room to report the missing creature.

He called his men to arms and told them to search the village and beyond for this creature. Some of the men shook their heads in fright and began to tremble.

"What is wrong with you? You are my chosen men. Are you men or are you weaklings?" The King gave the men his fiercest expression and waited.

One man stepped forward and replied, "We are men, King Kaposkaran. At least I am a man and I will do whatever you command of me."

"That's what I want to hear. If the rest of you do not agree, you will be executed in the village square. Do you dare disobey me?"

The men shook their heads in fear and responded as one, "We will do as you say, King Kaposkaran."

"That's better. Now search the village and beyond and go out into the forest of the Unknown Territory and find it. Bring it back to me. Here is a potion that you can put on your arrows. Shoot it and drag it back here quickly. It cannot have gotten far."

The men grumbled their discontent.

"You there, the man who stepped forward. You will oversee this mission. Make sure that you succeed."

"Yes sir," the man responded and backed away from the King along with the rest of the guards.

CHAPTER THIRTY-TWO

Quintal, the first Quintaroon, sat up suddenly from his cot. He looked around and smelled something familiar in the air. He rose and went to the window and looked around sniffing the air deeply. What is that scent? Why is it so familiar?

He knew that King Gateskin was watching him closely but he decided to take a chance and leave his hut in search of the scent.

He kept getting the same weird dreams of being something other than a man. He knew he had been a strange creature, as King Gateskin had told him. He didn't want to be that again. He felt confused and wanted to be able to sleep without these scenes playing around in his head. Maybe if he went outside, he would feel better with the fresh air and some exercise and at the same time find what was out there causing the air to smell like that.

Quintal opened his door and prepared to step out but found that he could not move. Something or someone was controlling his legs. He could not step out of the hut. He kept trying and began to sweat from his efforts. What was he going to do?

***

Gateskin watched Quintal try to leave his hut. He had put a spell on him that prevented the man from leaving his room. He turned to his wife and spoke softly, "I need to pay a visit to Quintal. It looks like he smells the other Quintaroon and wants to investigate. I cannot let him do that. He may turn into a Quintaroon again if he gets in contact with the second one. We just do not know if that could happen. I can't take a chance that it could, though."

"Yes, I agree. The saliva may trigger something in Quintal and bring out the creature again. We can't take a chance that it will join forces with the new creature."

"Make sure the children stay inside. I will put a spell on the house and our land here to keep it from coming closer in case my men miss it."

"You don't need to do that, Gateskin. I can handle that myself. But if I do, you will not be able to enter either unless you let me know you are near."

"All right. You do that. I will take care of Quintal. I keep forgetting the powers you have, my dear." Gateskin chuckled as he raced over to Quintal's hut.

When he arrived, he saw Quintal standing at the doorway trying to put his foot down on the threshold. His foot was in mid-air but he could not put it down.

"King Gateskin, please help me. Something is wrong with my legs. I cannot put my foot down. I was trying to go out for a walk."

"I know what you were doing, Quintal. I suggest you back away from the doorway and go to your table. I will come in to speak with you."

Quintal found that if he backed away from the door, he could move his legs again. He sighed in relief and sat at the table to wait for the King to join him.

"How are you feeling, Quintal," Gateskin asked as he sat across from the man and studied his features to see if there were any changes.

"I am tired and can't sleep at night or during the day. I keep getting these weird dreams that I am not a man but a creature. I know you told me I was once that creature, but I am no longer. Why doesn't it go away?"

"That I don't know, Quintal. You must be strong and keep fighting it. It wants to take over your body again. That is why it doesn't leave you."

"I understand. But I suddenly smelled something in the air that was somehow familiar to me. I don't understand what it is or why I recognize it."

"I do," Gateskin replied with a serious expression.

"What is it, King?"

"One of the villagers discovered some blood and guts and followed it to discover another Quintaroon like you were once."

"A Quintaroon like me?"

"Yes, unfortunately. We do not know where it came from or who created it. But I do suspect someone is responsible from Parotovina, where you came from a long time ago."

"Do you think that whoever made me created this new creature?"

"Yes, I do, Quintal."

"What are you going to do about it? Can you capture it and change it like you did to me?"

"My men are out there now trying to find it. Once they do, they will bring it to me. Then I will deal with it the way I did with you, in a peaceful manner."

"I see. Can I be there when you do that? I am curious to see it. I see it in my dreams and want to see it in the flesh."

"I don't think that is a good idea, Quintal."

"But why?"

"I will get you some food and a potion to help you relax. Don't worry about this. I will come back to see you soon. You will be told what happens to this creature."

"I…I…okay. I will wait. Can I go relieve myself while you are here? I can't leave on my own accord."

"Yes, I will take you to the outhouse safely and then back here."

"Thank you, King."

"I will have my men build you one inside so that you won't have to leave at all."

"Okay. But I do need to leave here to get some exercise and fresh air from time to time," Quintal pleaded.

"Of course. I will make sure that someone always comes with you to ensure your safety."

"Is it my safety that concerns you, King, or is it that of the village?"

Gateskin had disappeared without responding but had heard Quintal's words.

CHAPTER THIRTY-THREE

The men covered the woods in all directions without any sign of the Quintaroon. Spindle kept in contact with his fellow Sprites who watched from the treetops for any movement of the large creature. They did find some blood drops around a patch of grass that was free of trees. It appeared to be fresh.

Spindle came down to inspect it and responded, "It has been here and is probably close by. Be vigilant, men. It is quick and can come on you before you know it. Sprites are keeping watch over you and will alert me if they see it coming this way. Keep your weapons ready."

One man turned when he thought he heard something behind him. He screamed as the Quintaroon jumped toward him pulling him down.

Spindle flew over to the man and sent one of his small but powerful, potion-tipped arrows toward the creature. He hit it on the head and was prepared to hit it again but didn't need to, for it fell to the ground.

The man who had been attacked was shaken and had received a cut on his shoulder from the Quintaroon's claw. He had dropped to the ground not far from the Quintaroon.

Spindle called out to a few of the men to help the fallen guard and bring him back to King Gateskin right away.

He instructed the rest of the men, "Tie up the Quintaroon and prepare to drag it back to the King. We must leave quickly before it wakes up. I will put another arrow with the potion into its arm just in case but it will be difficult to move being a heavier weight."

The men nodded and got to work tying up the creature as tight as they could and attached it to a large tree limb as they began to drag it to the King's home.

Spindle sent word to the King's mind, "We have caught the Quintaroon but one of the men was injured and needs treatment immediately."

"Bring the man back right away. Make sure that you are not in danger of any more injuries from the Quintaroon. Put extra potion into him."

"Yes, King. I did that. I will see if my fellow Sprites can help by lifting the creature up off the ground a little to ease the burden of the men carrying it back so far. If we have enough Sprites, we just might be able to fly it over to you along with the injured man. We will work on that."

"Clever man you are, Spindle. That might work. I look forward to seeing you all back here safe and sound. I will prepare a place for the Quintaroon. See you soon."

"Thank you, King Gateskin."

"Thank you, Spindle. You are a good man."

Spindle blushed at the King's words and tried to cover up his face so that the men wouldn't notice.

CHAPTER THIRTY-FOUR

Solinara was in her workshop preparing the new food for the Catlings along with her brother, Hotenfaran. She turned when she heard Gateskin's voice.

"What is wrong, Gateskin?" She observed her husband's face that wore a pale tone.

"It appears that we do have another Quintaroon and it is heading this way. Spindle has used the potion to knock it out and with the help of my men and some Sprites it will be flown here shortly. We also have a man who was injured by the Quintaroon."

"I will take care of the man when they get here, but what are you going to do with another Quintaroon, dear?"

"That is a good question. I already alerted Quintal about it. He is safe in his hut and will not be able to come close to this one. I made sure of that."

"You can't put them together. Where are you going to put this one, Gateskin?" Solinara asked in alarm.

"I will build another hut further away from us and Quintal's. It will have to be fortified with spells to keep it contained. I don't know if Kaposkaran used the same formula to create it, meaning, used a man to form the base."

"How would he do it otherwise?"

"That's a mystery, Solinara, one that I intend to solve soon."

Before they could discuss this more, many Sprites were seen flying low and settling down with the Quintaroon and the injured man with the rest of the men who looked relieved to be on solid ground once again.

Queen Solinara took the injured man to her home to attend to him right away.

"King Gateskin, where do you want us to put this creature?" Mitteran asked as he saluted his king.

"Come this way and I will show you. I will need you all to begin building a hut as quickly as you can. I will help with a little magic to fortify it."

"Yes sir," the men responded and got right to work on gathering wood and supplies.

Spindle directed them and pitched in with his fellow Sprites, who carried some wood that was in the area to this site.

The Quintaroon began to rouse himself from the potion and struggled to fight his bonds. The men stepped forward and shot another arrow or two into the creature's body to subdue it.

Spindle bent down closer to the Quintaroon and poked it to ensure that it was out once again.

The Sprite jumped back in alarm when the creature shook and tried to open its eyes.

Mitteran pulled an arrow back and let it go into the Quintaroon with some extra potion. That finally worked to quiet the creature, much to the relief of not only Spindle, who was shaking, but also the men who were close by to see this happen.

Gateskin increased his magic over the building and spread strong spells to keep the creature contained there. Once it was finished the men lifted the Quintaroon once again with the help of the Sprites and placed it inside the hut.

They lay the Quintaroon on a bed there while they finished putting together a table and chairs. They put in an outhouse for the creature to use and stepped back to inspect their work.

"Nicely done, men!" Gateskin exclaimed as he spread more of his spells throughout the hut. He conjured up a meal and put it on the table along with a flask of juice for the Quintaroon to have once it woke.

"Let it sleep. When it is awake I will know, for I will be watching it closely through a window that I will keep open in my conference room. You can go back to your families. We are all safe, thanks to your diligence in bringing it here."

The men and the Sprites bowed to their king and left, leaving Spindle there with Gateskin.

"Thank you, Spindle. You did a commendable job once again."

"I didn't do it alone, King. You have good men who work tirelessly to do your bidding and my fellow Sprites. I am relieved that it is now contained. It shook me up a little when it almost came awake. I was much too close for comfort."

King Gateskin snickered, "Yes, I think you were, my friend. I think you were."

Queen Solinara called out to Gateskin, "Your man is doing well enough to return home. His scratches were minor and there is no infection."

"That is good to hear, dear. Thank you." Turning to Spindle the King instructed, "Get this man home safely so he can recuperate."

"Yes, King, right away," Spindle said as enlisted his fellow Sprites to help the man back home.

Hotenfaran came out of the workshop to join his sister, see the finished hut, and hear how the Quintaroon was doing.

"Is it asleep, Gateskin?" Solinara queried.

"Yes, for now it is. But I will be keeping an eye on it from my conference room."

"That is good to hear, dear. I don't want it anywhere near our children or the animals."

"No worries, Solinara. How did the food preparation go for the Catlings? Did you conjure something up for them?"

"Yes, Hotenfaran worked his magic once again. I couldn't have done it without him." Solinara gave her brother a grin and hug of appreciation.

"You flatter me too much, sister," Hotenfaran responded and rolled his eyes at her. "I had better get back to Procelina and Arubane. They are waiting to hear the news about the Quintaroon. It has spread throughout the land."

"Yes, I suspected everyone would be on the alert since I told them to be watchful," Gateskin replied as he sent word to the villagers that all was safe now that the Quintaroon had been captured.

"Well, it is better that way, King. They will be prepared if it escapes."

"I do not expect it to escape, if I can help it, Hotenfaran. Be on your way. Bring your family by this weekend for dinner. We have missed seeing you all."

"Yes, that is a wonderful idea, Gateskin. I should have thought of that. See you soon, brother. Give my best to Procelina and Arubane. I've missed seeing them."

"I will, Solinara. See you both soon."

Spindle waited to be excused as he flew around the King's shoulder.

"Oh, sorry, Spindle. You are relieved of duty now too. Go to your father. Give him my best, and tell him I will come by tomorrow to see how he is doing.""

"Thank you, King. I will tell him."

The King and Queen watched as the nimble Sprite flew back to his home in the tree after a job well done.

"I am fortunate, Solinara, to have so many good men and Sprites to assist me in this land. Let's go back home. The children are waiting to hear about everything, I'm sure."

"Yes, most definitely they will be antsy about the news if they don't already know it. They have good hearing and are probably keeping their ears to the walls now."

Gateskin chuckled and lent his arm to his wife as they headed back to their home a distance away from the Quintaroon's new residence.

They were unaware of watchful eyes as they walked along.

CHAPTER THIRTY-FIVE

Jelitza watched the King and Queen move toward a large house. She had followed her two cousins, Aharona and Navaeha, to this land to see what they had found so fascinating. She listened recently as her uncle had scolded the sisters about their travels to this land. She had waited for her cousins to leave Sovorotskina and stayed hidden in the forest near King Gateskin's home. She wanted to talk to him but would wait until morning. Her dragon, Verite, was snuggled up and fast asleep. She lay down in the folds of Verite's wings for comfort, warmth, and safety. The dragon had put them both under her protective shield so no one could see them.

Verite woke up with a start when she smelled something strange. She moved, disturbing Jelitza, who jumped up in alarm. "What's wrong, Verite? I was having a nice dream."

The dragon huffed and shook her head at her mistress. She hissed and sniffed deeply as she followed the scent further into the forest.

"Where are you going, Verite? We need to stay hidden until light."

Jelitza sighed and followed her dragon into the deep forest where it was darker and more difficult to travel with the tightly fitted copse.

Verite stopped ahead making Jelitza bump into her and shout, "What are you doing? Why are you going into this forest? I can't even see where I am going! Stop this right now. We need to go back. It doesn't look safe to stay here."

Jelitza could feel the air changing as it got more humid and a strong smell was permeating the air around them. She stopped moving when she heard a growling noise and spotted several eyes surrounding them.

"No, Verite. Do not go any further. We are being watched and possibly hunted."

Verite looked around and threw out her smoke as a screen to cover them. She breathed deeply taking in the scents around her and nodded.

"What do you smell, Verite? Are we in danger? What are those things?" Jelitza huddled closer to her dragon for protection as she waited for Verite to respond or do something to protect them.

She kept watching the eyes as they moved closer and materialized into strange-looking cat-like creatures with large jaws dripping with saliva as they kept their eyes on them.

"Verite, if you are going to do something, do it now!" Jelitza screamed as one of the cats reached out with its claws and tried to snatch her away from the dragon.

The dragon drew a large breath and blew out a stream of fire at the cat, burning its paw. It quickly drew back and licked its burn to ease the pain. The other cats withdrew likewise and waited.

Jelitza jumped up on Verite's back and clicked her heels into the dragon giving her a signal to fly out of there.

Verite shot out another stream of fire before lifting off and taking them out of the forest.

They flew back to the spot where they had slept under the cover of the dragon's protective shield.

"Why did you go there, Verite? We could have been a meal for all those cats."

Verite sighed and answered with her head bowed in shame, "I am truly sorry, mistress. I didn't realize that there were so many of those creatures. I smelled them and wanted to see what they were. They would make a good meal if I could grab one or two."

"No, you are not going back there, Verite. Do you understand what I am saying? We are here to see King Gateskin to find out why my cousins came here twice. There must be something intriguing to keep them coming back."

The dragon nodded and sighed before going back to sleep under cover once again.

Jelitza lay back down in the folds of Verite's wings and tried to sleep. She found that sleep was illusive, images of the creature trying to grab her kept her shaking and alert.

CHAPTER THIRTY-SIX

Spindle was surveying the borders once again after stopping by to see how his father was doing. He was relieved that his father was doing so well. It had to be the magic potions of Queen Solinara. He felt blessed to be King Gateskin's Head

Guard and to have the royal family as his friends.

His cheeks flushed as he thought of his favorite royal – Serena. She always did that to him – make him blush. But his blush was not like a human blush; it was from brown to green.

Coming out of his reverie, Spindle spotted a large object below as he flew over the borders of Skina Forest and the Unknown Territory. It looked like it could be those dragons and the two sisters again but they had already left. He flew down to investigate.

He landed on a nearby tree then down to the lower branches for a better view. The object was under a protective cover. He ventured a little closer and then stopped.

The object began to move and then sit up. Out of the cover stepped a woman, quite lovely, if he had to admit, with long dark hair that curled down onto her shoulders, but not as lovely as his Serena. He cleared his voice and spoke to her.

"Who are you and where did you come from?"

Jelitza looked up at the tree with a puzzled frown. "Are you a talking tree?"

"No, of course not. I am a Sprite." Spindle dropped down in front of her, startling her so much that she nearly fell over.

"I've never seen a Sprite before? Are you a stick creature?"

"Well, I guess you could say that. I am made of wood and live in the trees around Sovorotskina and elsewhere."

"Hmm, I see. What is your name? Do you have one or should I call you Sprite?"

"My name is Spindle. But you did not answer any of my questions yet. Who are you and where did you come from? Also, why are you here? Are you any relation to the two sisters who visited earlier?"

Jelitza smiled broadly. "Did you meet my cousins?"

"Yes, I did. But what is your name. Now I know that you are a relative and come from Dragonaria. Correct?"

"Yes, I am and I do. My name is Jelitza. I was curious to know more about why my cousins came here on two occasions. There must be something special here to attract them like that. They have gotten into trouble both times with their parents for leaving the island and traveling such a great distance as this."

"Oh, I did not know that. I feel sorry for them. Does that mean they will not come back? I really did like Aharona's dragon, Callum. He was friendly and not at all scary for someone as small as I."

"Yes, I agree. He is a kind dragon and nothing like Evander."

"Oh, yes, Evander is quite different. He tried to intimidate me."

"He did? What did he say to you, Spindle?" Jelitza was feeling less anxious now and moved closer to the Sprite.

"Well, he did say that he was nothing like Callum and that I better watch out because he couldn't be trusted."

"Oh, sometimes Evander is more bark than bite. Really, you shouldn't pay him any mind. I just ignore him and then he loses interest in bothering me."

"Do you have a dragon under there?" Spindle pointed to the large object that was behind her.

"Can you see her?"

"Well, I cannot make out what it is except that it is large and blurry and not part of the landscape."

"That's interesting. I didn't think anyone or anything could see us when we are under her protective cover."

"I'm sure not everyone can do that. But Sprites have keen eyes and can do and see things that others cannot."

"Well, that is interesting to know. Her name is Verite. She is kind and quite beautiful with silver scales that catch the light and sparkle."

"Wow! I would really like to meet Verite. Will she wake up soon?"

Jelitza leaned down and poked the screen to alert her dragon.

"Ahh, I was sleeping, Mistress! Are you in danger?"

"No, I am not. Wake up, Verite, and meet a Sprite. His name is Spindle."

"A Sprite? What is that?" Verite dropped her cover and stretched out showing off her beautiful silver scales that did catch the morning light that was coming over the treetops.

Spindle oohed and aahed mesmerized by the sparkling silver scales and the large dragon that was much too close to him. He stepped back a little and looked up into the large brown eyes of the dragon.

"Well, look here. It is a stick creature. You are called a Sprite? Well, you certainly are small."

"Nice to meet you, Verite. I may be small but I am powerful and have an important position with King Gateskin as his Head Guard."

"You do? That is quite a task for such a little fellow as yourself. Who is King Gateskin?"

Jelitza whispered in Verite's ear about King Gateskin and why they were there.

"Oh, right. Now I remember what you told me, Mistress. Sorry, I forgot. I am still a little groggy."

"Jelitza, you still didn't tell me why you are here. You missed your cousins. They already left hours ago."

"I know. I watched them leave and stayed here until light to meet the King and find out why they came here. I think it had something to do with the Medallion."

"Medallion? Oh, do you mean the missing Medallion that was buried many years ago?"

"I guess. I don't know much more than that. Why hasn't anyone found it all this time?"

"I don't know. I think Wizards came and went over the years to try to find it but were not successful. The rest of us don't care one way or the other about it. We don't need it."

A growl could be heard behind them making Jelitza jump forward, knocking Spindle down.

CHAPTER THIRTY-SEVEN

"What was that? I'm sorry, Spindle. I didn't mean to knock you over."

"It's okay, Jelitza. Are you all right?"

"Yes, I don't like that sound. It is frightening. One of those vile creatures tried to grab me."

"I agree, they are vile. They are known as Catlings and can be dangerous and problematic to our village. That is one of the reasons why your cousins came back - to help cull these creatures out. The Catlings have been trying to breach the borders. That is one of my jobs - to keep watch over the borders to make sure they don't get inside."

"What will happen if they do get inside? Will they come after everyone and everything?"

"Yes, unfortunately. That is exactly what they will do."

"How did my cousins help your king with them?"

"Well, as you know, dragons love to eat and are always hungry. Right?"

"Yes, I know mine is insatiable." Jelitza giggled as she looked at Verite's wide smile.

"Yup! I love to eat," Verite agreed.

"Well, King Gateskin summoned your cousins to come back to send their dragons into the UT to eat as many Catlings as they could and injure some to leave food for the rest."

"I see. But what is UT?"

"That is what we call the Unknown Territory."

"Well, it is not unknown if it has a name, is it?" Jelitza smiled.

"I guess so but that is what we call it just the same," Spindle grinned back.

"What are you going to do now that you are here, Jelitza?"

"I was going to ask you to help me by introducing me to King Gateskin. I would also like to find out more about the Medallion."

"Well, I can do that but I don't know if King Gateskin is busy. Let me fly over to his home and see if he is there to receive you. Okay? I'll be right back."

"Thank you, Spindle," Jelitza yelled to the Sprite as he flew away.

"This little creature can fly?" Verite asked in amazement.

"Yes, he can. He flew down to me from the tree while you were sleeping. He is quite cute, isn't he, Verite?"

"Cute? You call this stick figure cute?"

"Yes, he is cute. I like him. I think he and I will be good friends."

"Now don't do anything stupid, Jelitza. He cannot be your boyfriend or should I say stick friend?"

"We'll see. I think he likes me too." Jelitza chuckled to herself and watched the skies for her new friend to return.

***

Spindle landed at the doorstep of the King's home and flew up to knock as hard as he could on the door.

Serena was at the window and had seen him flying toward their house. She quickly opened the door and smiled at her special friend.

"Spindle, how are you? I wondered when you were going to come and visit me again. It's been a long time."

"Yes, I agree. But your father has been keeping me so busy and with my father's illness I haven't had too much time to spend with you."

"Well, why don't you come in and I will make us some tea and give you some delicious pie that I helped my mother bake."

"Mm, sounds great but I came to find your father to tell him that he has a visitor and another dragon."

"Another visitor and a dragon? Did this visitor come from Dragonaria too?"

"Yes, she did. I spotted her and her dragon as I was flying over to patrol the borders for the King."

"I see. I will tell Father. He is in the hut with the new Quintaroon."

"Do you think he would mind if I disturbed him to tell him about Jelitza and Verite?"

"Jelitza and Verite?"

"Oh, sorry. Yes, they are the names of the girl and her dragon."

"Girl? How old is she?" Serena wore a look of displeasure as she waited for Spindle to explain.

"Well, she is…um…I don't know how old. Maybe she is a little older than both of us."

"Hmm, I see."

"I'll be right back, Serena, as soon as I speak to your father. I promised to return to bring Jelitza and Verite back here to meet the King."

"You are not coming in for tea and pie?"

"Well, I can after I bring the visitors to your father." Spindle blushed and bent his head, not meeting Serena's saddened expression.

Serena turned suddenly, closing the door in Spindle's shocked face.

CHAPTER THIRTY-EIGHT

Spindle shook his head in disbelief at Serena's abruptness as he turned and flew over to the new hut for the second Quintaroon.

He couldn't forget the look on Serena's face as he had finally met her eyes. She was angry but at the same time disappointed in him. Spindle had never seen that expression in her eyes before with him. She always had a sweet look of …was it love or like for him?

He stood outside the Quintaroon's hut waiting for the King to answer. He knocked again and finally called out to King Gateskin, "King Gateskin, I need to tell you something. Do you have a few minutes to spare? Sorry to bother you."

The King opened the door and looked at Spindle. King Gateskin's face was sweaty and wore a look of exhaustion from whatever he had been trying to do with the creature.

"Are you all right, King Gateskin?" Spindle asked with concern.

"Yes, I am fine. It is tiring trying to reason with this creature. I don't know how it was created and if it even is a person inside there. It could be an animal for all I know. What can I do for you, Spindle? Are the borders secure?"

"Oh, yes, for now they are. I wanted to tell you about a visitor or visitors you have who want to meet you."

"Visitors? Where did they come from?"

"Dragonaria. A young girl and her dragon are here to speak with you. The girl is Jelitza and her dragon is called Verite."

"Why are they here?"

"She wants to know about the Medallion and why her cousins, Aharona and Navaeha, were here. I already explained about the culling of the Catlings. She was nearly caught by one she said."

"How did that happen? Did she go into the UT or did the Catling come into our land?"

"She landed inside the UT and escaped with her dragon."

"Well, that is good to hear she escaped and that the Catlings did not get through."

"Do you want me to bring her to you or do you want to go meet her?"

"I do not have time now, Spindle. I need to finish up with this Quintaroon and get it to sleep before I can leave it unattended."

"I understand. I will tell Jelitza you are too busy to say anything at this time to her."

The King watched Spindle fly away looking dejected. He called out to him, "Spindle, come back. I will see her and her dragon but I will go to them. I do not want to bring a dragon here again."

"Yes, I understand. I will wait here until you are ready to go meet with her."

Gateskin returned to the Quintaroon and placed a spell on it to eventually put it to sleep for now until he could come back after his meeting.

The Quintaroon looked at him and tried to speak but nothing intelligible came out.

"What are you trying to say to me, Quintaroon?"

"Ugg, grr, ahh."

"I don't understand what you are trying to say. I think I should give you a name. Would you like to have a name?"

The creature looked at the King and turned its head side to side in confusion. Gateskin spoke to it and said, "My name is King Gateskin. Your name will be Taron. Do you like that name?"

The creature just nodded and turned its head side to side again.

"I think you understand me, Taron. Now you must sleep to rest. I will leave some food for you on the table over there and some juice. When you wake, you will go to the table and eat and then lay down again. Do you understand?"

The creature nodded again and lay back on the cot and fell asleep after the King waved his hands over Taron one more time.

CHAPTER THIRTY-NINE

Spindle jumped up when the door of the hut opened and the King came toward him.

"I am ready, Spindle. Please bring me to the visitors."

"Yes, King. Follow me."

The duo flew to the area near Skina Forest where Jelitza and Verite were laying down undercover.

King Gateskin cleared his throat to get their attention.

Jelitza came out of the protective cover and nudged Verite to wake up.

"So sorry. I guess we both fell asleep again. We are still tired from our long journey."

"So, I see. I am King Gateskin, ruler of this land of Sovorotskina. Spindle has told me about you and your dragon."

"I am honored to meet you, King Gateskin. I am Jelitza and this is Verite." Both bowed to the King and only looked up when Gateskin told them to.

"I hear that you nearly had an altercation with a Catling in the UT."

"Yes, King, it was quite frightening. They are vile creatures, I must say."

"I agree, Jelitza. We have been having our issues with them. That is why your cousins came to visit again to assist me in culling out the herd of Catlings as Spindle has already mentioned."

"Yes, he did say that. But I also need to know more about the story about the missing Medallion that has been circulating on my island for many years. We don't know the whole tale of it though. Can you share more about that, King Gateskin?"

"There isn't much more to tell, Jelitza. It was buried by a Wizard over a hundred years ago and never been found even though others have tried. There is talk of it possessing powerful magic if it is found by a Wizard."

"What if it is found by someone like me without any powers?"

"I suspect that it would bestow upon you some powers."

"Really? What kind of powers?" Jelitza's curiosity was piqued and she waited anxiously for more information.

"That I do not know, Jelitza."

"I thought you were powerful in your own right, King. Who would know about this if you do not?"

"I can't really say. We haven't thought about this Medallion for years until your cousins came and asked about it."

"I don't understand. Wouldn't you or anyone else want to find it, especially before someone like me or my cousins do?"

"I would suggest, Jelitza, that you don't worry too much about it. It is not important. There are other things more important, like your life and safety."

"Why do you say that, King Gateskin? Wouldn't finding it add to my life and safety?"

"Not necessarily. It could harm you more than help you."

Jelitza furrowed her brow and became more intrigued after hearing Gateskin's words.

"I still don't understand," Jelitza shook her head and frowned.

"Sometimes we think we want to find something that appears, at the time, to be important. Once we find it though, we realize our mistake, that it really wasn't important enough to sacrifice ourselves."

"You really are confusing me, King. I won't know that until I find it though. Right?"

"That is correct. But you don't want to take the chance to search for something that you don't really need, do you?"

"How do you know I don't need it?"

"I see you as an intelligent young lady who has her whole life ahead of her with a strong, caring, friendly dragon who watches over her."

"That is true. I am young and Verite is my best friend and companion. She would do anything for me."

"Well, it sounds like you have everything you will ever need until you are old enough to find a husband and start a family."

"Maybe I don't want to do that. I would rather become famous and find the Medallion."

"Fame isn't always the best thing to attain, Jelitza."

"But you have it all, King. You are famous, have a loving family, so I heard, and a whole land of people who love and respect you."

"I have been fortunate and blessed. But that is more than enough for anyone to have."

"Well, maybe, maybe not. Can I stay here a little longer and begin a search?"

"Aren't you and your dragon hungry?"

"Well, maybe a little," Jelitza said as she looked at Verite who was salivating from hearing the word, *hungry*.

King Gateskin conjured up a couple of animals for Verite who gulped them down and burped in pleasure.

The dragon bowed deeply again to Gateskin and smacked her lips in appreciation.

"I guess that answers your question. Verite is always hungry. I could eat a little too."

"Follow me. I will take you to my home where my wife will make you something. You must instruct Verite to stay here under cover and out of mischief. Can she do that?"

"Yes, Verite listens to me and will obey." Turning to her dragon, Jelitza said, "Verite, did you hear the King? He wants you to stay undercover and be quiet and not get into any mischief."

Verite nodded and smiled, showing her teeth to Jelitza, King Gateskin and Spindle before laying back down and falling asleep.

CHAPTER FORTY

Spindle flew ahead as King Gateskin asked Jelitza, "Would you rather walk or fly to my home? It is a long walk but it would be quicker to fly there."

"I don't know how to fly without my dragon, King."

"I didn't mean that. I realize you don't fly. I meant that I would take you there myself. You need to hold on tight to my neck and off we go."

"Okay." Jelitza adjusted herself on the King's back and held on to his neck tightly in fear of falling.

Before Jelitza knew what was happening, they were up in the air and flying swiftly over the trees.

"Oh my! You do fly fast, King, almost as fast as my dragon," Jelitza said with a giggle. "It feels a lot different though since Verite's wings keep the wind off my face somewhat."

"Sorry about that. Are you okay?"

"Oh, I'm fine. It is exhilarating. Sorry to complain."

"Here we are. There is my home and my children in the yard feeding the wolves."

"Wolves? You have wolves? I've never seen a wolf before. We don't have any on our island."

"Yes, we have many. Your cousins were also surprised about the wolves. Come. I will introduce you to them and my children, of course," Gateskin chuckled.

The children looked up when they saw their father coming their way with a person on his back.

Serena was the first to come forward to greet him. "Hello, Father. We have a visitor?"

"Yes, this is Jelitza from Dragonaria. She is the cousin of Aharona and Navaeha."

"Oh, hi, Jelitza. I'm Serena, the oldest. You missed your cousins. They were here yesterday."

"Yes, I know. Nice to meet you, Serena."

"Do you have a dragon like your cousins do?"

Simon asked as he hurried away from the wolves to join his sister with Catalina on his heels, curious to meet the new visitor.

"Yes, her name is Verite. She is asleep in the woods a distance from here."

"Oh, can we see her?" Catalina asked with pleading eyes.

"Not now, Catalina. Verite is resting after having a meal," her father said.

"My name is Catalina. I'm the youngest, even though I am all grown up too. This is my brother, Simon."

Jelitza shook their hands and smiled. "Nice to meet you all. Maybe later before I leave you can meet Verite. I'm sure she would be happy to meet you all. She loves children and is kind, sweet and gentle."

"Really? Does she ever blow out smoke and fire like Callum and Evander?"

"Did they do that in front of you?" Jelitza asked in shock.

"Well, not really. But I think they could, especially Evander. He is fierce and scary," Catalina said with a sigh.

"Jelitza wants to meet the wolves. Do you want to introduce her, Catalina?" Gateskin asked, knowing how delighted his youngest daughter would be to do that.

Catalina took Jelitza by the hand and pulled her toward the wolves. She bent down and spoke to the mind of the leader of the wolves, Cantok and his mate, Notak. "This is our visitor, Jelitza. She comes from Dragonaria, an island far from here. She is the cousin of Aharona and Navaeha, the two women you met the other day. They had dragons with them. Remember?"

Cantok nodded and responded in Catalina's head.

"He said he is honored to meet you, Jelitza."

"Really? He said that? How do you speak to him, Catalina?"

"We correspond through our minds. I learned to do that after my sister did. Right, Serena?"

Serena smiled and nodded, "Yes, Catalina learned that on her own though. I already knew how to talk to the animals. It is one of my powers."

"Wow! You have powers like your father?"

Gateskin laughed at this. "They have powers I don't have. I can't speak to the animals but I can calm them or control them with other powers."

That is amazing!" Jelitza bent down and asked, "Can I pet their cubs?"

Catalina spoke to Notak and asked, "Can our visitor pet your cubs?"

Notak nodded and pushed the cubs toward Jelitza.

"They are so soft. Aren't they?"

"Yes, I was surprised about that too," Simon said as he petted one of them at the same time. "They are cute and cuddly too until they get bigger. Then they don't want to cuddle as much."

"How many cubs do you have? There are so many here."

"Too many at this time, Jelitza," Gateskin answered. "We need to build more huts and make more food to keep them happy and well fed."

"What happens if they don't get enough to eat?" Jelitza queried with concern.

"We don't want to find out," Gateskin said with a smirk.

"Let's get cleaned up and have some late breakfast or early lunch." Gateskin directed the group toward the house where Solinara was already at the door to greet them.

"Ahh, here is my beautiful wife, Solinara. This is Jelitza. She is the cousin of the other women who visited us yesterday."

"Hello, Jelitza. Nice to meet you. Are you hungry?"

"That is why we came back. We are all starving.

"No problem. I will whip something up for you. Come in, please and sit down."'

"We need to wash up since we have been with the wolves."

"Serena, take Jelitza to the washroom."

"Yes, Mother."

Solinara had a spread of sandwiches and soup laid out on the table when they all returned.

"What brought you here?" Solinara asked after everyone was quiet while they ate.

"I followed my cousins here and was curious about why they visited twice. I heard them talking about the Medallion."

"Oh, I see. Does the whole island of Dragonaria know about the Medallion?"

"I guess so. There isn't too much happening there, and we do like a mystery."

"Yes, it is a mystery to us too. But we have lost interest in it. It has been too many years. We really don't care to search for it. Others have tried and been unsuccessful."

"Yes, I learned that from King Gateskin. But I am really intrigued by the tale and wanted to try and find it."

"Why do you want to do that, Jelitza?"

"I don't know. I guess I'm just curious to see what it can do. It's magical, I heard."

"Yes, it is magical but it is not good magic. It may be Dark Magic, the worst kind and the most dangerous and difficult one to control. You don't want to get anywhere near it."

"Do you really believe that?"

"Of course. We know that since the Wizard who buried it wanted to get rid of it because of how dangerous it was. He didn't want anyone else to have it for that reason."

"Why is Dark Magic bad?"

"Well, it is known to control a person so much it can turn that person to pure evil."

"Oh! That is not a good thing."

"No, it is not. You are young and do not need to have this Medallion. It will only cause you trouble and ruin your life."

"Well, maybe I won't search for it." Jelitza said, disappointed.

"Good. I'm relieved to hear that." Solinara finished her lunch and began to clear the table as she met her husband's eyes and nodded.

***

Back on Dragonaria, the sisters searched for Jelitza. They hadn't seen her all day and wondered why she wasn't close by spying on them as usual.

CHAPTER FORTY-ONE

Back in Parotovina King Kaposkaran mulled over what his wife had done and what King Gateskin had said about the new Quintaroon being in his village.

He had to do something to get it back and possibly the original Quintaroon too. He would have more power if he had two creatures under his control.

The King summoned his guards to his conference room and asked, "Have you seen the guard with the funny nose anywhere? If you find him, send him to me right away."

"Yes, King. I'm not sure which one you mean. What is his name?" one guard inquired.

"I don't know your names. I only recognize you by your distinctive characteristics."

"Hmm, I see, Sir. I will look around for a guard with a funny nose."

"Don't be insolent with me, Towhead!"

"What?"

"You heard me. You have light blond hair and therefore you are a towhead."

"Oh, okay. Do you need anything else, Sir?"

"No, go on your way and find him."

Towhead bowed out of the conference room with the other guards wearing puzzled looks on their faces.

"Do you believe that? He doesn't know any of our names! He called me Towhead!"

"Who do you think he means with the funny nose?"

"I don't know but it could be one of a few men. We should scatter around the village and on the outskirts to see if we can find him."

Back in the conference room, King Parotovina bristled over the insolence of his guard. How am I supposed to keep track of everyone's name with over a hundred guards?

That guard has not returned, he thought. Something must have happened to him. How am I supposed to find out how to rid the village of this moss which is still here? That is not, however, as important as the Quintaroons are now. I will have to send more men out to Sovorotskina and bring back the Quintaroons. Once I have them under my power, I won't need anything else. I could gain control of all of Noella Province. He chuckled to himself as he called for his meal.

The guards searched the whole village and outskirts of Parotovina for any guards who could have ventured there without success. They returned to tell the King that they were not successful in finding the guard with the funny nose.

They feared retribution from their king if he was unhappy with their futile search.

When they stood in front of the King as he was eating his mid-day meal, they bent their heads and sighed deeply before Towhead spoke for them.

"We searched everywhere, King Kaposkaran, but have not found this missing guard with the funny nose you mentioned. He is not here. Maybe he went outside our village into another village."

"Hmm, that could be the case. That is why you will go searching other villages until you find out what happened to him. If you do find him, bring him back here right away. Also, I need some of you to continue to Sovorotskina and find the Quintaroons."

"Quintaroons? There are more than one, King?"

"Yes, there are two now. You must find them and bring them back. Bring your spears with the sleeping potion on the tips and make sure he is sleeping before you attempt to drag him back here. I do not want to lose all of you."

"Lose all of us?" the guard asked in a quivering voice.

"Yes. Don't you remember how dangerous this creature is? Now you will have two to bring back."

The guards looked at one another dumbfounded and proceeded to draw straws to choose who would search for the missing guard while the rest of them searched for the Quintaroons.

CHAPTER FORTY-TWO

Gateskin took Jelitza back to her dragon who was now awake and looking around for a snack. Verite stopped in her tracks when she sniffed the air and knew at once that her mistress was returning. She promptly lay back in the grass and pretended to sleep.

"Verite, are you sleeping again?" Jelitza poked the dragon once she found her under her protective cover.

"There is always time for a nap, Mistress." Verite arched her back and stretched out her wings as she looked at King Gateskin who was standing behind Jelitza.

The dragon's mouth began to water as she waited in hopeful anticipation for a tasty creature from the king who was smiling broadly at her, fully aware of her need.

Gateskin nodded to Verite and once again conjured up two furry creatures and laid them at the dragon's feet. He winked at Verite and backed away as he watched the creatures disappear into the dragon's large jaws.

Verite gulped them down, licked her lips and smiled, satisfied. The dragon bowed in thanks to Gateskin and returned his wink with one of her own.

"Well, I guess you are full now, Verite," Gateskin said with a chuckle.

Verite nodded while she picked her teeth with her claws to remove some of the fur left behind.

"I will put a spell over you and your dragon, Jelitza, so that you will be able to fly home quickly under cover. I do not want any of the other villages to be able to see you and get alarmed."

"I appreciate that, King Gateskin. I was a little worried about being shot down."

"That could be possible with our powerful arrows and potions. But no need to worry. If they don't see you, they can't shoot you out of the sky."

"That's good to know. Thank you and your family for the kind hospitality. I will give serious consideration to what you and your wife told me about the Medallion. But I know that one of our own practices Dark Magic."

"One of your own?" Gateskin asked in shock.

"Unfortunately, yes. It is the oldest sister of Aharona and Navaeha. She is called Elowen. She lives on the other side of the island away from all of us. The three sisters do not get along ever since Elowen started using Dark Magic."

"Hmm, I see. Does Elowen know that you and her sisters have come here?"

"I don't know. I certainly won't share that with Elowen. But there is also…"

"What, Jelitza? What were you going to say?" Gateskin inquired, feeling unnerved.

"Well, there is a friend or now a foe of Aharona and Navaeha. That's Mianna. She was the sisters' best friend. They did everything together. But they had a falling out and now Mianna is friends with Elowen. We haven't seen her since then."

"I suggest you be careful and do not share that you have been here or anything about the Medallion."

"Yes, of course. I understand. I will make sure that Aharona and Navaeha do the same."

"Good. Be on your way and be alert just the same even with the cover spell. Go directly home."

"I will, King Gateskin. I don't know if I will be back again, so thank you again for everything."

"My pleasure, Jelitza."

Jelitza jumped onto Verite's back and they flew into the air causing trees to sway and branches to bend in the wind.

Gateskin spread his hands over them as they gained speed and height and soon disappeared.

Gateskin hurried back to his home to inform his wife of what he had learned about Dark Magic on the island of Dragonaria.

CHAPTER FORTY-THREE

Gateskin did not find his wife in the house but in her workshop where she was working on making more food for the wolves and a special potion in food for the Catlings to keep them at bay.

Solinara looked up when she heard the workshop door open and her husband standing there looking disturbed about something. She only hoped that the visitor and her dragon were now gone.

"Gateskin, what is wrong? You have a funny look on your face."

The King sat down on a bench and sighed. "There is trouble ahead. I can feel it, Solinara, and it is not good."

"What trouble is good, Gateskin? I haven't discovered any that is good so far," Solinara smiled, trying to ease her husband's stress.

He explained to her about the Dark Magic on Dragonaria.

"That is not what I expected you to tell me. I thought it was a problem with the girl and her dragon not wanting to leave until they looked for the Medallion."

"No, I don't think she will be back. You discouraged her with Dark Magic."

"Well, that is a relief to hear. I don't want to see them back here for any reason. She is a nice enough young lady but we don't need anyone digging on our lands and destroying our fields to look for this elusive Medallion."

"Yes, dear, I agree. But we have bigger problems if this Dark Magic comes here. We have had enough to deal with from Parotovina with Queen Beregina casting a spell that nearly took all our lands out with that moss."

"We will deal with whatever comes our way, Gateskin. Don't worry about something that may never come to pass."

"You always have a way to calm me down, Solinara. I don't know what I would do without you and your counsel."

"That's right and don't forget it either," Solinara laughed, clearing the apprehension in the air. "I could use your help in getting this food to the Catlings to keep them satisfied enough not to try to break through our borders."

"What do you need me to do, Solinara?"

"Fly this over to the UT and drop it in an area that has Catlings visible. They will come to it and bring it back to their caves."

"I will get Spindle to help me. He can get several of his fellow Sprites to carry some of the food further into the forest."

"That's good. Well, I need to wash up and get dinner started. I didn't realize it was getting so late." Solinara bent down and kissed her husband's cheek before leaving.

Gateskin smiled at her, sighed, finally stood up and gathered a few buckets with the food for the Catlings and flew to find Spindle.

Spindle saw the King heading his way and met him. "What do you need me to do, King?"

After Gateskin's instructions, Spindle flew with one of the buckets to the trees bordering the UT and called out to the Sprites. "Please take this bucket and come back for more food. You need to drop this into the UT for the Catlings. It is a special potion in the food created by our Queen Solinara to keep the Catlings inside the UT and satiated. There is more to be dropped so ask the other Sprites for help."

The Sprite nodded and took the bucket with the help of a few other Sprites as they began to drop the food to the hungry Catlings who quickly ate it up.

While the other Sprites finished this task, Gateskin shared what he learned with Spindle about the Dark Magic on Dragonaria.

"This is not good news, King Gateskin. What are you going to do to prevent this from coming here?"

"I don't know yet. But I will be working on some spells of my own to keep us safe."

"I am not worried. I know how powerful and capable you are to keep us from danger. You have been doing this for a long time. If you need me to do anything to assist you, please do not hesitate to call on me."

"I know I can always depend on you, Spindle. Thank you. Please share this with Mitteran but no other guards just yet. I will tell them if the time comes to do that. I think we are safe for now."

"Okay, I will do that. Mitteran is a good man and an immense help in all tasks you have given us."

"Yes, that I know, as are you, Spindle. I need both of you on my side as my counsel."

"You have us, King Gateskin, whenever you need us. I know Mitteran would agree on this."

Gateskin nodded as he said, "Thank you. I must get back to check on the animals and work on my spells. Say 'hello' to your father for me. I will visit him again soon."

"I will. He enjoys your visits and is feeling much better and getting stronger by the day."

"Good to hear."

Gateskin flew back to the wolves' hut and checked to see that they were all safe and fed. He next visited the barn where he looked in on Milly the cow, horses, chickens, and goats. All seemed to be settling in for the night.

He spread a spell over the area to keep them safe from any predator that may come their way. He knew that the wolves would not venture here but he was still aware of the Catlings and what they could do even though they were being fed to feel satiated more quickly.

He called out to his children and Serena came out of the workshop with some more food for the wolves.

"You should finish with your chores and get inside. It is getting late and your mother will be calling you to come in soon."

"I was on my way there after dropping off this food for the new mothers in the wolf huts," Serena stated as she looked at her father's furrowed brows deep with worry.

"Where are your siblings?"

"They are already inside. I told them I would take care of the wolves."

"Okay. Good."

"Are you all right, Father?"

"I'm fine, Serena. I have a lot on my mind now, but nothing to concern you."

"Oh, well, if you need me for anything, I am here."

"I appreciate that, Serena. I will remember that. I know I can always get help from you with all your powers. It is daunting at times how powerful you all are," Gateskin said with a smile that calmed his furrowed brows a little.

"Yes, it is, Father," Serena giggled with relief when she saw her father's face appear serene again. She would mention this to her mother when she went in for dinner. She watched her father turn and head back to the house deep in thought.

Serena could feel something in the air coming their way. She hurried to feed the wolves and go inside. She must share this feeling with her parents.

Who knew what was coming next?

CHAPTER FORTY-FOUR

Deep inside the UT a few of the Parotovinan guards searched for the missing guard. They felt something drop from the sky and looked up. What they should have done was look down and around them for that view of the sky was the last thing they saw.

The hungry Catlings attacked the guards from behind as they dragged them away into the forest. The guards never knew what attacked them for they were devoured quickly by the ravenous Catlings.

The only things left were the guards' clothing that was scattered, shredded in pieces all over the forest floor. Once the Catlings finished, they left to find a place to sleep until their next meal.

The tainted food sat where it landed until they would find it later.

The Sprites who dumped the food had watched the Catlings consume the guards and flew swiftly back to report the slaughter to Spindle.

Spindle was surveying the borders when the Sprites found him to share the horrific news.

"What? You mean that the Catlings didn't eat the food but ate some guards instead?" Spindle replied in shock.

"Yes, Spindle. We couldn't believe our eyes. The guards were devoured so quickly that one minute they were standing and the next there were only piles of shredded and bloodied clothes!"

The other Sprite added, "It was horrendous to see. I felt sick to my stomach and still do!"

"Did you see where the Catlings went after that?"

"We think they headed deeper into the forest to rest now that they were full."

"Yes, I bet that is what they did. Thank you for being so observant. Did you see how many men died?"

"We think about three or four. They wore the uniforms of Parotovinan guards."

"Thank you. I will relate this to King Gateskin. Keep an eye out for any more activity from the Catlings and whether they eat the food you dropped."

"Yes, Spindle. We will be on alert."

Spindle nodded to his fellow Sprites and flew over to find the King

Gateskin was discussing the situation with Solinara when they heard a knock on the door. Looking out they saw Spindle flying around, clearly agitated about something.

"Spindle, is everything all right on the borders?"

"Yes, but there is a problem with the Catlings. Two of the Sprites reported this…." Spindle continued to relate the situation.

"What? Why were the Parotovinan guards in the UT? Are they crazy? Don't they know how dangerous it is there with the Catlings?"

"I don't know, King. I asked myself those same questions after I heard this."

"I will have to report this to King Kaposkaran. He must have sent them there for some reason."

"Maybe he was looking for the Quintaroon, King."

"Yes, that is quite possible, Spindle. Thank you. You don't have to stay here. Why don't you go back home but keep watch from time to time on the borders as usual."

"Yes, Sir. I will do that right away." Spindle bowed as he backed away and flew from Gateskin's home."

"What are you going to do, dear?" Solinara inquired with a worried frown.

"I must call Kaposkaran. That is the only thing I can do and report this. He will be looking for his men."

"I will go check on the children and make sure they stay inside until daylight. We can't be too careful."

Gateskin nodded and went into his conference room to summon Kaposkaran. It wasn't going to be a pleasant thing to share with the King.

He opened the Conference Channel and waited for Kaposkaran to appear. It took several minutes as usual to reach this king. King Kaposkaran of Parotovina was always reluctant to answer a call from King Gateskin.

CHAPTER FORTY-FIVE

King Kaposkaran was in conference with a couple of his guards who were out of breath as they entered his state room. They were disheveled and sweaty from their journey.

"Where are the rest of you? Did you find the guard with the large nose and the Quintaroons?"

"No, no, we didn't, Sir! What we found was…" the guard couldn't go on. He was so distraught that he fell to his knees and cried.

"What is wrong with you! Are you an imbecile?" the King looked at the man with disgust.

The second guard stepped forward and explained in a voice that shook and stuttered, "We…we stumbled upon some of the Catlings. Unfortunately, four of our m... m... men were eaten by them before we could do anything to stop them. We ra…ra…ran for our lives all the way back here. There was so ma…ma…many of these creatures there that we didn't think we would escape."

"Where are the rest of the men? Are they still looking for the Quintaroons?"

"Yes, we separated so we could look for the guard you requested we find while the rest of the men went a different way to search for the Quintaroons."

King Kaposkaran shook his head in disbelief. "Leave me now. Go home and get cleaned up. You are a mess and smell bad. I will call you if I need you again."

The King listened to a call coming in through the channel that King Gateskin always opened to reach him and the other rulers.

"What does he want now? I have enough to deal with," he said in exasperation. He clicked on the channel and accepted the call.

"Ah, there you are, Kaposkaran. I have important news, though it is disconcerting to share, you need to know this."

"What is it, Gateskin?" Kaposkaran asked with impatience.

Gateskin explained about what the Sprites found in the UT.

"Yes, I just found that out from some of the guards who returned unscathed by the attacks. Well, they are not completely unaffected. They were frightened out of their minds," Kaposkaran harrumphed in disgust.

"I'm sorry about your men, Kaposkaran. It is an awful situation for you to explain this to the men's families."

"Ha, I do not do that. The other men will relate this news to the families. I have better things to do than waste my time crying over something I cannot control."

"I see. Well, you do what you must, Kaposkaran. I would not do that, for my men are sacred to me and my saviors in time of need. They are like family to me."

"I don't feel that way, Gateskin. I am not you."

"Yes, I can see that. Well, I send my condolences to all the families of these poor men who were taken that way. It was a horrendous way to die."

"Yes, yes. I know. What else did you want? I need to get back to my business at hand. I am waiting for more men to return unless the Catlings ate them too."

"How many men did you send into the UT and why?"

"It is none of your concern, Gateskin. I had business for them to take care of."

"Were you looking for the Quintaroon by any chance?"

"I…I…maybe I was. So, what of it?"

"You will not find either Quintaroon in the UT. They are in my safe keeping. You need not worry about them. They will not harm anyone if I have anything to say about them."

"What makes you think you have anything to say about them? They are my creations and mine alone. I want them back immediately."

"We will not discuss this now, Kaposkaran. You need to deal with your losses first." Gateskin disconnected the Conference Channel and closed it down so no more messages could get through. He had enough of Kaposkaran and his sadistic nature. The man was a monster. He felt sad for all the men under Kaposkaran's control.

CHAPTER FORTY-SIX

The next morning Gateskin woke up to the sound of the wolves howling in warning.

He got dressed and went out to see what it was that was bothering them.

He only prayed it wasn't the Catlings getting through the borders.

Serena poked Catalina who ignored her, rolled over and went back to sleep. Serena went into Simon's room to wake him to warn him something was happening out in the yard.

"What's going on, Serena? I was having a good sleep. It's too early to get up, isn't it?"

"Listen, don't you hear all that howling? It's the wolves. They are in distress and are giving a warning to the rest of the pack and us too."

"Yeah, I did think I heard something but I thought it was in my dream."

"Get dressed and come outside. Father may need some help. I will go speak with the wolves to see what is wrong."

"Be careful, Serena!" Simon yelled to her back.

Catalina jumped up from her bed when she heard her brother's voice. She peeked in his room and saw him getting dressed.

"Get out of here, Catalina! Don't you knock first before entering?"

"Sorry, Simon, but I heard you yelling at Serena. What's wrong?"

"I guess you didn't hear the wolves howling either?"

"Well, I did hear something but I was too tired to go find out what it was. Serena poked me and I ignored her and went back to sleep. I'm still tired."

"That's what you get for staying up reading all night."

"I had to read that book that I found about the Wizard. It was fascinating. There are some spells in there that I want to try sometime."

"Where did you find the book?"

"I'll tell you another time."

"I would not recommend trying any spells unless you check with Mother first, Catalina. Get dressed. We may need your assistance with the wolves. Something is seriously wrong."

"I will. Be out in a second or two," Catalina called back as she raced back to her room to change.

Outside their home Gateskin checked over the borders around the wolves' enclosure without spotting any problems but the wolves still were agitated.

Spindle flew over to where Gateskin was standing by the border of the UT and Skina Forest.

"What's going on, King?"

"That is what I would like to know. I have checked all the borders around the wolves' huts and now further away.

There is no break in the spells covering the area."

"I agree. I will fly further away and see if I can spot anything coming this way."

"Yes, that would be helpful, Spindle. Let me know what you find if anything."

Several of the other Sprites were doing the same thing when Spindle arrived in the UT forest. Catlings were seen roaming around as usual but not too close to the borders. They were looking up though as if they had seen something there.

Spindle turned his attention to the sky. He spotted a large black thing in the sky that was heading their way.

He flew back to Gateskin and reported what he saw.

"Did it look like a dragon, Spindle?"

"It could be or it could be a flying guard from Parotovina. There are some who can fly and have powers like those of years ago who were instrumental in capturing our peoples, during the time of the Taken Ones."

"Ah, yes. I think you may be right. Send a warning to all the Sprites to keep watch and report whatever they see."

"I expect this visitor is heading this way to see me."

CHAPTER FORTY-SEVEN

The Quintaroons were restless in their respective huts. They sensed something was happening outside. They each tried to open their doors and leave their places but were stopped in their tracks by the spell that Gateskin had placed there.

Quintal, the first Quintaroon was used to this and tried everything he could to move past the door. He sniffed the air and sensed something evil was close by. There was also another scent that was familiar to him, to his past. He now suspected it was the other Quintaroon.

The second Quintaroon, now known as Taron, was eating the meal that Gateskin had left him when he heard the ruckus outside. He opened his door but could not venture further. He did the same thing as Quintal, sniffed the air, and sensed something that he did not understand. It smelled like him.

Quintal went from window to window to see if he could see what was happening out there. Taron was doing the same things almost as if they were on the same wavelength.

Their huts were separated by Gateskin's house which blocked their view of each other. The king had planned it that way to keep them further apart and unaware of each other. Evidently, their strong sense of smell detected what Gateskin had not considered.

Quintal called out to King Gateskin, "King, I need your assistance here. What is going on outside?"

Gateskin heard Quintal and went directly to his hut to calm him down. He did not want to have this man turn into a Quintaroon now with everything else that was going on.

"Everything is all right, Quintal. Do you need anything? Food, blankets?"

"No, I just want to go outside and take a walk. I need to stretch my legs. You can't keep me here forever? I am not the evil creature now that you say I was before."

"I realize that, Quintal. When I think you are ready to live amongst us that way, I will let you know. Until then, you will stay here." Gateskin closed the hut door and walked away.

The King visited with Taron next knowing that this creature was still inside the man who now appeared stable. It may even sense Quintal was nearby.

Taron was standing in the doorway of his hut when Gateskin came to visit him.

"What is going on, King Gateskin?"

"Ahh, good to hear that you can speak. There is nothing to worry about, Taron. How are you feeling? Are you hungry? Is there anything you need?"

"No, I finished eating. It was delicious. Thank you. I am just concerned about what is happening outside. Can I come out to get some fresh air? I am tired of being cooped up here."

"I understand how you feel, Taron. Everything is all right outside. Nothing for you to worry about. When I think it is safe enough for you to go out, I will let you know. You are still in the beginning stages of changing back to a man. Your transformation is not yet complete. You may be a danger not only to yourself but to others too."

"I am feeling better and am no longer having cravings like before. I don't understand what happened to me. Once minute I was searching for food, and the next two guards pulled me into the castle in Parotovina to see Queen Beregina. Did she do something to me?"

"Unfortunately, she did, Taron. That is why I must watch over you and ensure that you are normal again before I allow you to go outside. You must understand, I have children of my own besides all the rest of the villagers to watch over."

"I see. I don't want to cause any problems. I am thankful that you are trying to help me. I just need..." Taron didn't finish his words because Gateskin had disappeared.

The black cloud was descending and heading into Sovorotskina. The other rulers had noticed this same cloud and were trying to contact Gateskin through the Channel Spell.

Solinara was in the kitchen when she heard the clicking sound of the Channel. She went into the Conference room to see who was trying to contact her husband.

CHAPTER FORTY-EIGHT

Gateskin met the black figure who was coming his way. He was surprised that it was a woman as she landed near him.

"King Gateskin? I am Elowen, sister of Aharona and Navaeha. I know they came here to visit on a couple of occasions. I hope they were not a bother to you."

"Elowen. I did not know they had another sister. What brings you here to Sovorotskina?" Gateskin kept his countenance, not giving her any indication that he had heard of her from her cousin Jelitza for fear that harm would come to the young cousin.

"I wanted to meet you, King Gateskin, since my sisters spoke so highly of you and your beautiful land. It is quite green, like nothing I have ever seen before."

"Yes, I'm sure it is. Your island must be more colorful with all the dragons. Why don't you have a dragon?"

"I find that I can fly faster than any dragon can without the drag of their wings and tail. Dragons don't particularly like me anyway."

"Why don't they like you, Elowen?"

"I don't know. Maybe it is because I won't let them control me. I think they fear me for that reason. I am stronger than they are in mind and spirit."

"I see. Can I offer you some refreshments?" Gateskin changed the subject.

"Maybe a drink would be nice. I am quite thirsty." Elowen's eyes spotted the wolves who were roaming back and forth protectively in front of their huts with their families safely inside.

"Let me take you to my house. My wife is there waiting to meet you, I am sure."

Elowen ignored his words and walked closer to the wolves who were growling and looking menacingly at her as she approached.

"I wouldn't suggest that you get too close to the wolves. They are most protective of their families."

"Where did you find these creatures, King Gateskin?" Elowen asked as she crept closer still.

The leader of the wolves, Cantok, growled louder in warning to Elowen as he stared at her with his glowing yellow eyes.

Serena was close by and spoke to Cantok in his mind, "Don't attack this visitor. She is just curious. She will not harm you or your family, my family will not allow it."

Cantok listened and nodded but did not back away and kept his eyes on the woman who came closer to look at him.

"Can I take one of these wolves back to my island as a souvenir, King Gateskin? I know my father would be pleased to have one. We do not have anything like this on our island. I would make sure that it is always kept safe from the hungry dragons."

"I cannot do that, Elowen. The wolves are our friends and I have promised to always keep them safe in return for their friendship and protection too."

"Hmm, I understand. They are intriguing creatures, most powerful and menacing. I like that," she smiled at Cantok but her smile did not reach her eyes which stayed set on the wolf to intimidate it.

Cantok backed away and disappeared into his hut to check on his family.

"Who is this lovely young lady, King Gateskin?"

"This is my oldest daughter, Serena, and my son, Simon and youngest daughter, Catalina."

"I am Elowen. Nice to meet you all. I hear that you met my sisters, Aharona and Navaeha."

"Yes, we did. A pleasure to meet you too, Elowen," Serena responded as did her siblings.

"I think we should go inside and have some refreshments now. My wife, Solinara, is waiting." Gateskin guided the visitor to his home. He looked back at Serena and told her in her mind, "Be careful of this one. Take your siblings and go into your mother's workshop until she is gone. I don't trust her."

"Yes, Father," Serena said to him as she whispered to her siblings what he had said.

Solinara was at the door waiting for them to come in. Gateskin did the introduction and they all sat at the table where Solinara had put a pot of tea and some biscuits she had made that morning.

"This is kind of you, Solinara. Nice to meet you and your family. You have a lovely land here."

"Thank you, Elowen. I wasn't aware that there was another sister from Dragonaria. We are slowly meeting the whole family."

"So, it seems that way, Queen Solinara. I have a question for you both. My sisters have been whispering about a magical Medallion that is supposedly buried here on your land."

"Yes, that is the tale that has spread for many years. We do not know if it even exists."

"Oh, I think it exists. I can feel its powers emanating through the land. It is here somewhere and I plan to find it."

"I don't think that is a good idea, Elowen. We cannot let you do that to our land. We had our lands nearly destroyed before by others who came here to search for it."

"You may not have any way to prevent me from doing this, King Gateskin."

"What did you say, Elowen?" Gateskin stood up from the table and towered over her as his eyes took on a glowing appearance that would frighten anyone in the land.

Elowen drank her tea and finished her biscuit as she stood and excused herself. "I take my leave. I can see I have overstayed my welcome. Nice to meet you both and your children. I will be on my way back home."

Gateskin did not respond but backed away from the table to give Elowen room to leave. He escorted her to the door and watched her look over one more time at the wolves before flying away.

He watched the skies as the black cloud of her cloak disappeared into the horizon. He wasn't happy with this latest visitor and expressed his concern to his wife who said, "I agree, Gateskin. I only hope she doesn't come back and try to do a search. I fear for our people and animals, especially the wolves. She took a liking to them. Do you think she will be back to steal one?"

"I hope she doesn't, but I will be ready if she does."

"I need to tell you, Gateskin, that the other rulers have been trying to reach you through the Channel Spell. Maybe it is time to warn them of this danger."

"Yes, I planned to do that."

CHAPTER FORTY-NINE

Gateskin went into his conference room and opened the Channel Spell that showed the anxious faces of his fellow rulers of the Province of Noella. The rulers never used their titles when they spoke to one another this way, only their first names.

"Gateskin, we have been frantically trying to reach you. We saw a black cloud heading your way and feared it was Kaposkaran and his minions coming to destroy your land," King Cavelan of Votovia explained.

"I appreciate you trying to reach me, Cavelan. I was planning to share this information with you. It was not Kaposkaran or any of his men but another visitor from Dragonaria."

"How many visitors have you had from this place called Dragonaria?" King Noderan of Amora asked in surprise. He was unaware of any visitors from this place.

"Sorry, I did not share information about them with you. King Cavelan of Votovia is the only one who knows of their visits. I thought it was time to share this one because of the danger she may bring to us."

"Danger, a woman you say?" The Healers of Merona asked in shock. They ruled their village since there was no Wizard there to do that. They were powerful in their own rights though.

Before Gateskin could respond to them, King Zuri of Merlina queried, "Maybe you should start from the beginning, Gateskin, so we will all be caught up with this news. Who were the first visitors?"

Gateskin explained to them about the two sisters, the cousin and then the eldest sister and why they visited in the first place. He also told of his problems with the Catlings and how the two sisters helped cull out the herd to an extent.

"Well, you certainly have been busy, Gateskin," King Zuri responded with a heavy sigh. "You should have asked for our assistance. We are stronger together, my friend."

"Yes, we are. We will need each other, for this latest visitor may return."

Gateskin continued to explain the latest visitor and the danger she could cause with her Dark Magic and how she wanted his wolves, leading to her warning about searching for the Medallion and that no one could stop her.

Noderan stated, "We will need all the magic we can conjure to fight her if she does come back here. We must be ready for anything."

"Yes, I agree, Noderan. We will need our Wizards to work their magic along with our own to ensure the safety of Noella Province."

"Have you told Kaposkaran about all this?" Cavelan asked.

"No, unfortunately, I cannot talk to him about anything. He always gets upset about everything. He never takes anything I share with him seriously. He is only concerned with losing his Quintaroons."

"Quintaroons? You mean there are more than one now?" The Healers asked in alarm.

"Yes, there are now two. I have both in their own huts under a spell to keep them inside. They cannot escape. They are both coming along and almost completely back to being men again." Gateskin continued to explain how the latest Quintaroon came to his village.

"Well, that is a relief," Cavelan said with a sigh. "I wondered what happened to the one that terrorized all of us as he flew overhead. Do they know about each other?"

"For now, they do not know each other exist. Don't worry about them. I have them under control. What we must worry about is this visitor named Elowen and her Dark Magic. She will be back to search for the Medallion. I never thought it was important to find this Medallion. But now maybe it is time to find it and destroy it before she can find it and use it against all of us."

"I agree," Noderan stated.

"Yes, I do too," Zuri said.

"I also," Cavelan responded in a firm voice.

"Of course, we agree with all of you," the Healers added.

"That is good to hear. We will need to share this with Kaposkaran whether he wants to listen to us or not. If anyone feels like they want to take on this task of sharing this information with Kaposkaran, please do so. He will not take my calls now since we had words recently," Gateskin explained.

"No problem, Gateskin. I will take on the challenge since I am the closest to his village," King Noderan offered.

"Thank you, Noderan. He may listen better to you," Gateskin sighed in relief.

"I will help you do the explaining, Noderan," King Zuri added. "We may need both of us to convince him to listen to reason. He can be stubborn and determined in his own opinions of what is important."

"I appreciate your help, Zuri. It may take two of you. But please be careful of not only him but also his wife. She is dangerous and known to use Dark Magic."

"Yes, we remember the moss. I think it is still covering some of Parotovina," Noderan stated, with a sigh.

"I think we may have just found out how to offer him something in return for meeting with us to discuss this situation," Zuri said with a grin.

CHAPTER FIFTY

Back on Dragonaria, Jelitza watched as Elowen flew down in front of Aharona's and Navaeha's huts. The cousin stayed hidden in the bushes for fear of being seen and burned to a crisp from the Dark Magic of Elowen.

Aharona and Navaeha were aware of their sister's visit but hesitant to find out what she wanted. They hadn't seen her in months. Elowen had stayed on her own part of the island without contacting any of the family. They feared her use of Dark Magic and were careful what they said to her now.

"Well, sisters, how are you doing?" Elowen smiled but not with a warmness that reached her eyes.

Aharona did not return the smile but nodded and asked, "What brings you this way, Elowen?"

"Oh, I was just passing through from a visit to your friend's land."

"Friend? What friend?" Aharona asked in alarm, fear covering her face and evident in her eyes.

"Oh, you know. The one that you visited a couple of times already."

Navaeha exchanged worried glances with her sister before responding, "Did you go to Novella Province?"

"Why, yes, I did, little sister. It was just lovely and so green."

"Did you meet the King there?" Navaeha asked, hesitantly.

"Yes, we had some tea and pleasant conversation. I met his wife and children and the remarkable wolves. I would love one of them or maybe two so they could procreate here on our island. I could really use them in my spells. Imagine what I could do with their power and majesty?"

Aharona shivered at the thought of what her sister could do to these animals. She only hoped that King Gateskin would keep them safely contained.

"Would you like to know what King Gateskin and I discussed?"

"Umm, not really, Elowen," Aharona turned to go back inside her hut, pulling Navaeha with her.

"Where are you going?" Elowen asked with urgency. "I am not finished with you both."

Aharona looked back and stated, "I am not interested in what you want to do with or without your magic. All I can say is you better stay far away from Noella Province and King Gateskin. He is more powerful than you can ever imagine and will do anything to take care of his land and people."

"Is that so, Aharona? What do you know about power? What powers do you have?"

"I don't need powers to be happy, Elowen. Maybe that is what is missing in your life – happiness."

"What are you talking about, Aharona? I don't need anything or anybody to make me happy. I am happy with myself and my magic. That is all I need."

"Well, then you should be on your way back to your part of the island and away from us." Aharona went back into her hut and pushed Navaeha ahead of her safely inside.

"This is not the end of our conversation, sisters. I know all about the Medallion and I plan to find it and no one will stop me." Elowen flew away to her own hut and never looked back.

Jelitza came running out of the bushes and knocked on her cousins' door. "Aharona, Navaeha, let me in!"

Aharona opened her door and stared at Jelitza. "What are you doing here? You just missed Elowen. You could have been injured. She does not like you very much and wouldn't want you around here."

"I know, that is why I hid in the bushes over there. She never saw me. I heard everything she said. I can't believe she went to Noella Province and met the King and his family. I wonder what he thought of her?"

"Yes, we know. We were there too. I don't like the fact that she went there. Her plans are dangerous and may harm someone. We need to do something," Aharona said as she looked at Navaeha.

"What about me? I can help you too. I went to visit the King also," Jelitza shared with a grin.

"You did? When did you go there and why?"

"I wanted to see why you were going there. I know about the Medallion and its power too. It is Dark Magic. Queen Solinara told me."

"That is why Elowen wants it. We must stop her. I don't mean you, Jelitza. You are still too young to get involved. Stay here and report to our father if we do not come back."

"What? No, you are not going without me."

"Listen Jelitza, you must stay here. How will our father know where we disappeared to?"

"Are you leaving now?"

"No, tomorrow after we think this through. Elowen will return there soon, I am sure of it," Aharona stated, with a frown of concern.

"Yes, I agree," Navaeha said. "We must help Gateskin and his family. Also, we must ensure that Elowen doesn't steal any wolves."

CHAPTER FIFTY-ONE

King Noderan and King Zuri met at the crossroads of their lands and took a wagon into Parotovina to meet with King Kaposkaran. They had sent a messenger ahead there to set up an appointment with King Kaposkaran.

The guards at the gate of Parotovina had a message to let them enter. Another few guards were standing nearby to greet them and bring them to the castle to King Kaposkaran's conference room.

King Kaposkaran was seated at a long conference table deep in thought as they were escorted into the room. He never looked up but pointed to two chairs in which he wanted them to sit.

King Noderan cleared his throat and waited for Kaposkaran to acknowledge them. King Zuri did the same a few seconds later.

Kaposkaran finally looked up and asked, "Why are you here?"

"Sorry to disturb you, King Kaposkaran, but we have news of utmost importance to share with you," Noderan began.

"What could be more important than what I have to do?" Kaposkaran asked in an impatient manner.

"We all have important issues in our own lands to take care of, Kaposkaran," King Zuri pressed without using the title king.

"Fine, share what you need to tell me and make it quick. I have a lot on my mind right now. I am still dealing with this annoying moss. I can't get rid of it no matter what I do."

"Well, we have a few spells that will take care of that for you. If you listen to what we have to say first, we will take care of it and make it disappear for good," Noderan said as he met Zuri's eye and nodded.

"Well, spit it out! I don't have all day! This moss keeps growing and spreading," Kaposkaran urged them on as he bristled with annoyance.

Noderan poked Zuri to continue. "I don't know if you were aware of some visitors from an island called Dragonaria. There are three sisters who live with their family. They all have dragons, well, except the oldest sister who uses Dark Magic. She is what you would call a Dark Fairy. She is quite dangerous and has threatened to use her magic to find the Medallion that was lost over one hundred years ago."

"Lost Medallion? Ah, yes. I remember hearing about that. I never believed it though since no one has been able to find it. I would gladly search for it if I believed it was real."

Zuri mumbled his thanks to Noderan.

"What did you say, Zuri?"

"Oh, nothing. I was just clearing my throat so I could explain more."

"Well, go on. What is this all about and how does it concern me?"

Zuri picked up the explanation, "Well, it is evident that this older sister will be back to search for the Medallion but she threatens all of us with her Dark Magic. If we allow her to come back and use it and possibly find the Medallion, then that is the end of us all. She will take over all our lands and rule. We need to band together to prevent this from happening."

"Hmm, I see. What do you plan to do? Does Gateskin know all this already?"

"Yes, he does. We told him we would share this with you and get your support to fight back all together," Zuri answered.

"If we band together, we are stronger than apart. We need every village ruler to help rid our lands of this Dark Fairy," Noderan explained.

"What about her own island? Won't they protect her and fight back?"

"No, her own family is against her magic and will not support her. They fear her," Zuri responded.

"I see. What do you need me to do?"

Noderan clarified, "Well, we need you to support any efforts we put forth such as spells to keep the Dark Magic from spreading, something like keeping the moss at bay."

"I haven't been able to do that though. How can I stop Dark Magic?"

"We know that your queen can do that. She used Dark Magic to create the moss," Zuri inferred.

"Well, I do not want her to do that anymore. It caused too many problems; one I still can't get rid of. Are you going to help me banish this stuff or are you going to bore me to death with this nonsense?" Kaposkaran stated, with vexation.

Noderan nodded to Zuri and said, "We will certainly do that if we get your assurance that you will do as we say about assisting us in keeping the Dark Magic away."

"Okay, I agree. I will speak with Beregina and make sure she will use it to keep us safe. Now will you please do something about this moss. It's driving me crazy. My animals keep eating it and falling asleep."

Zuri spread his hands over the land when he got outside the castle with Noderan and Kaposkaran with him.

Kaposkaran watched in awe as the two rulers recited their spells in a whisper as they spread their arms and waved them back and forth over the lands that were covered in green.

"Look, it's disappearing!" Kaposkaran cried out in wonder.

Zuri and Noderan kept the spell spreading until all the moss had stopped moving and turned brown and shriveled.

"You will need to burn it, and cover your mouth and nose when you do it. It will no longer be a problem once you do that."

"Okay. I will have my men take care of it. I can't believe you did that! How come I can't do that? Can you share that spell with me?"

"Not now. If we need to, we will later. For the time being, keep alert to any visitors flying in from the south."

"Some of my men told me about a black cloud passing over here. I didn't pay too much attention to it because it quickly disappeared," Kaposkaran said nonchalantly.

"If you see it again send out an alert to Gateskin's Channel Spell. He will alert the rest of us. We must be vigilant. She will return with a vengeance," Zuri announced with a stern expression.

"Okay, don't worry. I will. Now you must be on your way back home. You don't have too far to go, being next door." Kaposkaran summoned his men to first escort the visitors back to their wagon and then burn the vestiges of browned moss. He went back inside his castle, looked out the window and admired his land as it was becoming clean once again.

Zuri and Noderan shook their heads in disbelief as they left the castle to go back to their wagon and head home. They were not too happy with the hospitality of the King or should they say, lack of it.

CHAPTER FIFTY-TWO

King Zuri called Gateskin to report what had transpired amongst him, King Noderan and King Kaposkaran and added, "Not even a 'thank you' was uttered in response to our clearing out his village. I guess we should not be surprised. He will not be much of a help to any of us."

Noderan was listening and added, "I agree. He will be more of a deterrent to us. I only hope that his wife doesn't do anything strange again like create another moss disaster."

"I appreciate what you both did. Thank you for trying. At least he must have been relieved that you got rid of the moss," King Gateskin said.

"I think he was pleased about that. We left him admiring how clean his village now looked and that his animals were waking up," King Noderan responded.

"Haha. I can imagine. Well, let's not worry about him. We need to concentrate on the rest of our villages and people to keep them safe. I will need several of your men to begin digging for the Medallion. We must find it soon and destroy it before someone else finds it."

"How can we destroy something so powerful?" King Zuri asked with hesitation.

"I am working on that. I will need your Wizards to begin spreading some netting down all over the province to protect the people and animals. This netting will keep the land from being destroyed when we begin digging. It should keep the land from breaking apart and creating holes. Once we dig in one spot we cover that spot over quickly, thus the netting to fill in the holes. We don't want anyone falling in and getting injured," King Gateskin stipulated.

"Yes, I understand. We will get them to work on that right away. Should we send the Wizards over to you to do this or can they do it from afar?" King Zuri asked.

"They can do it from afar if that is possible for them. I will have my Wizards do the same from here. I also have some powerful people here that I will be using besides my own family's powers. We will need all the help we can get to do this quickly and under cover."

***

Gateskin flew to the hut of Henno and Jenara, the powerful couple who escaped from Parotovina and sought asylum in Sovorotskina. He knocked and waited a few minutes before Henno peeked out at him.

"King Gateskin, how nice to see you. I'm sorry we haven't stopped by to thank you again for our lovely hut and the land. We have been busy tilling the soil and raising crops and animals. What can we do for you?"

Jenara opened the door further and welcomed the King in. "We are honored by your visit, King Gateskin. Is there some way for us to repay you for all you have done for us?"

Gateskin sat down after he was invited to have some tea and biscuits.

"That is why I have come by. I do need your help with an important issue."

"Whatever you need, we are available to help," Henno stated as he waited to hear more.

Gateskin explained about the latest visitor from Dragonaria and how she wanted to search for the Medallion to aid in her use of Dark Magic.

"I did hear about this Medallion in the past even before we came here but never thought much about it since. Do you believe it exists?"

"Yes, I feel its power but haven't located it. I know it is somewhere on my land. I will need everyone to help in locating it as quickly and safely as possible and disarming it of its power."

"I see. Do you know how much power it contains and if there is a way to contain it?"

"Yes, I do know it has Dark Magic that is more powerful than my own power, that is why I need your help and my Wizards too to contain it."

"Do you want us to go out into the fields and begin searching right away?" Jenara asked.

"Yes, I have already started the process of digging and laying out a spell with netting to cover everything that we are doing to keep eyes in the sky from seeing anything."

"That is wise, King Gateskin. If that woman comes back, she will know what you are doing and come to make trouble."

"Yes, that is why we must act quickly. Come to my conference room. I will be gathering all the villagers who have any kind of power to assist me. I need to contact my brother-in-law Hotenfaran and his wife Procelina now. Go on to the conference room; Solinara will be there to greet you. I will be there shortly."

Gateskin stopped at Hotenfaran and Procelina's hut and was about to knock when the door opened. Hotenfaran stood there and nodded at Procelina and they came right out to follow behind Gateskin. Gateskin did not have to say a word, they knew what he needed for they had conversed in their minds.

"I hope you have some ideas, Hotenfaran. I need all the assistance I can obtain from you and Procelina."

Before his brother-in-law could answer Arubane stepped out of the hut and followed them.

"Where do you think you are going, son?" Procelina asked with a stern expression.

"I want to help you. I do have many powers that will be helpful to you. I heard what you said in your mind. I know all about this Medallion and will be the one to find it."

"Is that right?" Gateskin asked as he looked closely at the boy who had been adopted by Hotenfaran and Procelina from the age of five. He was a little older now and much bigger.

"I don't want to be rude, King Gateskin, but you need me." Arubane stood taller and smiled at his parents and the King.

"I believe you, Arubane. Come with us."

Arubane proudly stepped forward and led the way to the King's home.

CHAPTER FIFTY-THREE

Solinara was there to greet all the villagers, her brother, sister-in-law, and nephew as they arrived. She made them comfortable in the large conference room that grew larger to accommodate everyone and supplied drinks, biscuits, and other food.

Gateskin rounded up every villager who had any kind of power, and then stopped by to see Spindle and Mitteran to explain what needed to be done. "You are to oversee the digging and search for the Medallion. Meet the villagers who are coming from the other lands to help and get them started in plots assigned on the map." Gateskin handed the map to them. "I will be meeting in my conference room with my Wizards and others who I will be sending your way soon."

The two head guards nodded and flew to the site marked on the map.

The King then led the villagers with powers to his home and seated everyone before beginning his instructions. He had also summoned his Wizards to come right away. They were there in a split second after his summons and stood along the side of the conference room walls until needed.

Gateskin gazed at all the people who were gathered there and sighed. "There is much to be done. We must find the Medallion before a person from the island of Dragonaria finds it and uses it to increase her Dark Magic."

He explained how she had come to his village and expressed a desire to find the Medallion and that no one would be able to stop her.

He heard gasps from all those gathered there and shocked expressions as they all waited to hear more.

"Yes, she is a dangerous person and one that I do not want to return here. We need to work together using our skills and powers to the maximum. If there is anything you can do that you have not shared with me yet, please feel free to do so now without retribution."

The King waited for anyone to respond. He looked at everyone seated there and noted shakes of heads and heard 'no' from many.

"Well, I guess then we must use what we can. My Wizards are here to cast spells to help us with our work. We will be digging in all Sovorotskina and will need everyone to do their share of the work whether it is manual or with powers to find this Medallion. Do you all understand what I am asking?"

Several nodded in agreement while others answered, "Yes, King Gateskin."

"I have a map of what areas each of you will be taking for your search. Spindle and Mitteran are already out there with some of the other villagers from neighboring villages who have begun the search. We need to complete this task as quickly as we can and then cover up the areas we have already searched. The netting will help keep the land level and safe. If you find anything at all you must let me, Spindle or Mitteran know immediately. I have flags laid out for you to use when you do find something to mark the place."

"Is this Medallion dangerous to touch?" one villager asked, in hesitation.

"This I do not know but you must not touch it in case it is. I will have my Wizards nearby to handle it with their powers."

"What will you do with it when we find it, King Gateskin?" Henno asked.

"I will be conferring with my Wizards about that. I also have the other kings at the ready if we need their Wizards to help."

Jenara spoke up, "We could bury it in a cave in Ailylene Mountain and use a spell to conceal it."

"Yes, that could work. I will be working with Solinara, Hotenfaran and Procelina to come up with something that would be effective."

Arubane stood up and cleared his voice. "I could help you with that, King. I know many spells that my birth parents taught me and more now from my new parents that would work."

Hotenfaran and Procelina beamed with pride at their son's suggestion.

"I believe you could work wonders, Arubane. I will keep you in the loop when I need to have a spell to do that."

Arubane grinned and nodded. "I am ready, King, whenever you need me."

This young boy did have many powers that even astonished Gateskin when he was discovered amidst the sheep during their sojourn in and out of Parotovina rescuing the Taken Ones. Arubane had transformed himself into a black sheep that had stood out amongst the white sheep and then, before their eyes, had changed back into a boy.

Even Arubane's adoptive parents did not know how to do that and they had myriad powers.

"Now, are there any other questions before I assign you a place to dig?"

Gateskin glanced around the table at each person and waited for them to answer individually before saying. "No? Okay, then let's get everyone a place to work on the map."

Once everyone was out on the land, they worked the rest of the day on their areas digging then covering up if nothing was found before moving onto another plot.

Gateskin gathered his family along with Hotenfaran, Procelina, Arubane, Henno and Jenara, and his Wizards to begin to create spells to contain the Medallion once found.

They discussed which ones would be most effective to contain it and how deep it would have to be buried if it could not be destroyed outright.

The King mulled over what they had created for spells and looked over the landscape of Sovorotskina.

"You may be right, Jenara, about burying it in Ailylene Mountain. We may be able to use a spell to open a fissure there and then cover it with another spell. We have several spells here that would work."

Jenara nodded with a smile. "I think any one of these would work, King Gateskin."

Solinara added, "We also do not know if by digging this artifact up if we will unleash its powers automatically, Gateskin."

"I am worried about that. That is why the Wizards must be vigilant and watch over the land for any sign that it is being unleashed."

The Wizards stepped forward and whispered to Gateskin, "We will go out to the land now and use a spell or two to cover it so it cannot unleash any magic when it is found. We will take care of that, King."

"Yes, please go out there now in case anyone is getting close to finding it."

Gateskin opened the Channel Spell to alert the other rulers of the lands that he was actively searching now.

All the rulers relayed that their Wizards were busy preparing spells in case they were needed to contain the Dark Magic if it somehow escaped.

"I appreciate your support. I will keep you abreast if it is found. My Wizards are out on the land now and watching over the digging to ensure that everyone is safe. If this Dark Magic does escape, we have no idea if it can destroy everything in its path. We must be prepared for anything."

King Cavelan of Votovia agreed, "I have seen what Dark Magic can do with the Moss Spell created by Queen Beregina and how it continued to grow in Parotovina. It took all of us to stop its growth."

"Yes, that is why we must work together. I don't want to see something like that happen again."

King Noderan said, "It was a tough spell to break but we did it more than once in all our lands. We will tackle anything that comes our way this time too."

"Thank you all. I need to get out in the fields now to see how things are progressing. I will talk to you later when we know more."

Gateskin closed off the Channel Spell and everyone left the room to follow him outside.

CHAPTER FIFTY-FOUR

All over Sovorotskina the land was being searched without any results. Gateskin visited all corners of his village and thanked the diggers for their efforts. He told them to take a short break and get something to drink and eat. They shook their heads and continued to work. Gateskin spoke to Spindle and Mitteran about how much of the land had been covered so far.

"They are almost up to Ailylene Mountain. They will be there by tomorrow. We are finding some strange things in the ground as we get closer to the base of the mountain. It looks like some sort of metal dust."

"Metal dust? That is strange. Let me get the Wizards here to check that out."

The four Wizards bent down to look at the substance in question, picked it up, felt it between their fingers and even sniffed it and tasted it before responding, "We think it is part of the mountain that has flaked off due to erosion. It is not valuable but more like an igneous rock dust from a volcanic eruption," Marno, Head Wizard explained.

"Yes, I see that now. If we dig closer to the base of the mountain we will find more. Maybe that is where we will find the Medallion," Gateskin stated, hopefully.

"That is possible, but we will have to blow up the side of the mountain and repair it so that it won't completely cave in and undermine our land all around it," Marno added

"Of course, that could happen. I don't want anyone injured if we have to do that," Gateskin said with a frown.

"We will keep an eye out for any problems, King," Spindle and Mitteran said in unison.

Gateskin nodded and surveyed the land and the people who were digging.

The four Wizards, Marno, Fortag, Wassor, and Tornak gathered some of the stone dust and put it into cloth bags they had tied to their waists to bring back for closer inspection. They planned to use a spell or two on it to see if there was any reaction, positive or negative.

Gateskin observed the Wizards gathering the dust and asked, "Will you be testing this dust for any Dark Magic?"

"Yes, also other things, King. We may find something that will lead us to the Medallion."

"Good. Let me know what you find." Gateskin bent down to gather some for his own testing before moving on to another area. He walked to the mountain and looked closely at the base and the land around it. He felt for any vibrations coming deep inside the dirt. He used his vision to look deep inside the land around the base. There was nothing there that was sending off any vibrations or chemical reactions.

It was getting darker now and time to stop the digging and let his people go home to rest for the next day.

Gateskin called out, "Everyone stop digging. It's time to go home for dinner. We will get back to this tomorrow. Please come back early after daybreak and we will begin again. Thank you for all your efforts today. We will be successful tomorrow, I am sure."

Groans of aching diggers could be heard as they headed back to their homes dragging their shovels with them.

Gateskin waved his hands over all the villagers to ease their pain and tiredness to ready them for the next day.

Sounds of relief could be heard as the men turned to look at their king and nodded their thanks. They stopped dragging their shovels and shouldered them as they walked home with backs straight and strong once again.

***

Back at the workshop Gateskin opened the bag of rock dust and shared it with Solinara and Hotenfaran who were ready to test it with their spells.

The four Wizards were doing the same thing with their bags of dust.

There was a spark of something that flew out of one bag of dust and escaped the eyes of the Wizards who were intent on their testing. It flew up to the ceiling of their hut and stayed there.

CHAPTER FIFTY-FIVE

It was just daybreak back on Dragonaria. Aharona and Navaeha were getting ready to return to Sovorotskina to assist Gateskin with the search. They were also going to warn him about the dangers that their eldest sister could wrought on him and his people.

Jelitza was closely watching her cousins as they packed their dragons with a few things before jumping on their rides. She had readied her own dragon, Verite, who was waiting for her to get up onto the saddle for their long journey. She would wait a short time before following them so as not to be detected. She knew they would force her to return home.

What Jelitza did not know was her cousins were fully aware of her intention to follow them. They had given up telling her not to come but would have to make sure their young cousin was always safe.

They feared that if Jelitza stayed behind that Elowen would force Jelitza to relate what they were going to do in Sovorotskina. Their cousin would be safer with them than alone on

Dragonaria. They couldn't share any of this with their father for he would forbid them from going back.

The two sisters discussed what they would do to help the King. Even though they did not have powers like the King did, their dragons had many powers that would be helpful.

Aharona whispered to her dragon, Callum, "Listen, we will need your help when we get back to Sovorotskina. There is danger there with this Medallion. We don't know where it is but Elowen plans to search for it. We must help King Gateskin find it and destroy it once and for all."

Navaeha was sharing this also with her dragon, Evander, "You need to be strong and powerful to assist King Gateskin find this Medallion that has Dark Magic."

"Dark Magic?" Evander queried as he turned his head to look at Navaeha.

"Yes, Elowen wants to find it. We can't let her do that. She would use it to destroy everyone and everything."

"I see. Yes, she is a dangerous one. How did she become like that when you are nothing like her nor is Aharona?" Evander asked in surprise.

"I don't know. She has never been a happy soul and I guess she let the darkness in and liked it."

"Who would want that?" Evander inquired with a frown that wrinkled his scales pushing them up further.

"I know I would not. Will you be ready to help us?"

Evander answered with a grunt and nod.

"Good. We need you and Callum."

"We will take care of both of you," the dragon responded.

"You may have to take care of the three of us."

"Three?"

"Yes, Evander. Jelitza is on her way here too. She is following us a distance back. She doesn't realize that we know she is there."

"I don't know if Verite is as strong and fierce as you and Callum are."

"I think Verite can hold her own. She can wrestle better than ever now. She has been working on that to keep us in line," Evander chuckled.

"That's good. Then we have three strong dragons to back us up. That's good to know."

Aharona was listening in on her sister's conversation with the dragon and butted in, "I guess we are plenty ready to help King Gateskin then."

"I agree, Aharona. I should have known that you would be listening. Do you agree about Jelitza? Do you think she will be safe?"

"Well, with three fierce and powerful dragons to back us up, we can't fail. Can we?" Aharona guffawed.

Callum and Evander smiled wide in pleasure and picked up speed as they lifted their huge wings to propel them forward.

***

Elowen was preparing some spells to use for her return to Sovorotskina. She had almost finished the last one when she heard the fluttering of wings over her part of the island.

She looked up to see two specks in the distance and another one further behind. She grabbed her spyglass and looked closer.

"Where do they think they are going? I hope they don't think they will beat me to finding the Medallion!" She said disgruntled. "They have much to be surprised by once I get there."

Elowen quickly finished up her spells and put on her flying cloak and looked around to make sure all her belongings were safely locked up in case someone came skulking around.

Mianna watched her from a short distance and waited for Elowen to leave before moving away. She planned on sharing what she saw with the King and Queen since Elowen did not keep her in the loop or invite her on the journey.

CHAPTER FIFTY-SIX

King Gateskin rose before daylight and grabbed a quick bite before going outside to feed the wolves and the barn animals. They were just rising too. Milly mooed when she saw Gateskin coming her way. Her tits were full and dripping as he looked under there. Gateskin grabbed a pail and pumped out as much as he could to give her some relief and grabbed several eggs to bring back to the house for his family to have for breakfast. He dropped off the milk and eggs in the house and headed out to the digging sites.

When he arrived Spindle and Mitteran were already there organizing the men into new plots. They were getting closer to the mountain range and more rock dust was being uncovered.

A fluttering of wind was felt as they all looked up to see three black spots in the sky heading their way.

Gateskin went to where the spots were landing and saw the two sisters and their cousin jumping off their dragons and coming toward him. Jelitza had finally caught up to her cousins after they had waved her forward to join them as they were landing.

"What are you all doing back here?" Gateskin asked in surprise and impatience.

"Sorry if we are a nuisance, King Gateskin, but we came to help you. We know about our sister Elowen and her Dark Magic and how she threatened to search for the Medallion. We can't let her do that. If she finds it, she will destroy you all and your lands," Aharona stated, urgently.

"Yes, we are here to help you, King Gateskin," Jelitza jumped in, eagerly.

"I see. Almost the whole family is here together. I don't think it was a good idea for you to be here. We are trying to find the Medallion now before anyone else does. I don't know how you can help us."

"We don't have powers like you and your family do, King, but we do have powerful and fierce dragons," Navaeha added.

The three dragons grunted and looked as fierce as they could as smoke floated around their heads in concentric circles.

"How can they help find the Medallion?" Gateskin asked, clearly confused.

"Well, I think we should let them look for it. You would be surprised how talented they are," Aharona stated, smugly.

"Do you know something that I don't, Aharona?"

"Well, I could tell you a little story but it might take too long to do. Maybe we should let the dragons fly over the area and see if they can spot anything there."

"I don't know about this. Let me warn my people first that your dragons are not here to eat or kill them. They will be frightened since my people have never seen such creatures here," Gateskin stated, urgently.

"Okay. We will wait until you do that before unleashing them," Aharona replied with a wink.

Gateskin flew over to the area and called down to his people to warn them, "Please do not be alarmed. You will see three dragons flying over this area. They are here in peace and will not harm you. Step aside and let them fly over. They are here to help us find the Medallion."

Spindle flew up to meet Gateskin and asked with deep concern and curiosity, "How are they going to help us, King? This is quite strange."

"I agree with you, Spindle. It is a strange thing. But we must let them look. Maybe they have powers to see what we do not."

"Okay, King Gateskin. I am quite curious to see what they can do. I guess we do need all the help we can get."

Gateskin went back to the sisters and their cousin and nodded to them. "Give them the command to search. I have asked my people to step aside until they are through. I would be quite surprised if they did find it."

"Of course, King. But you would also be very pleased and thankful," Navaeha added.

"Yes, I would," Gateskin agreed and flew back to the area to watch the dragons in action.

CHAPTER FIFTY-SEVEN

The villagers scurried away from the area and hid behind trees close by. They watched in wide-eyed wonder as the huge creatures flew high above where the digging was taking place.

The three dragons were a beautiful spectacle to watch in action as their scales glistened in the sunlight and appeared to be gold, silver, and rainbow-colored.

The three young women stood with Gateskin as they observed their dragons dip and sway over each plot of land. The incredible creatures' eyes glowed and gave off a light that pierced the soil and dug holes at each spot they touched.

Aharona whispered to the King, "Do you see how they can cover so much more than your men in a shorter time. They are also sensitive to metal and will cause it to glow making it easier to spot."

"Hmm, I see. The rock dust is glowing and lifting out of the soil. It has metal properties that are being affected by the burn of the dragons' eyes."

"One day I will share the story I mentioned, King, about what the dragons can do. They are multi-talented in many ways."

"I can see that, Aharona. I would be interested in learning about what else they can do."

Aharona smiled and nodded to her sister. "I will be happy to spend some time with you, King, and share what our dragons can do. You would be amazed at their gifts."

As the dragons got closer to the mountain range more rock dust glowed and floated above the soil and dropped back down forming into solid pieces once the dragons moved away from it. They flew closer to Ailylene Mountain and scanned the base and moved slowly up its side.

The villagers were in awe as the mountain began to glow brighter as the dragons reached the peak. Rock dust was flying around and lifting away from the mountain as the dragons concentrated on the peak. Before they could move to the top there was a gust of wind that caused dust to fly around and blind everyone including the dragons.

Gateskin waved his hands over the dust and pushed it down so he could see what was causing the disturbance in the air. What he saw was not what he had expected.

He called out to everyone to cover their faces with a cloth to keep out the dust until he could fly up to see what was causing the wind storm. He didn't explain what he had seen to anyone as he flew closer to the black cloud that was hovering over the mountain.

He met the cloud and spoke softly so as not to alarm his people below. "What are you doing, Elowen? You need to leave now."

"Why would I do that? I will not leave until I have it in my hand."

"You will leave here now!" Gateskin's eyes glowed almost as bright as the dragons' as he focused his gaze on Elowen forcing her to turn away.

She shook her head and tried to gain her composure as she used her powers to turn her own glowing eyes on the King.

Gateskin was ahead of her and covered his eyes with a spell of his own as he gathered more spells to send to counteract hers.

Neither was successful in gaining power over the other but they did not give up and used every spell they could create to throw at each other.

The dragons flew closer to see what was happening. When they could make out what was in the dust cloud, they whispered amongst each other and flew closer and behind Elowen to send their own glowing eyes on her back.

Elowen could feel heat on her back and turned to see what was causing this. When she saw the dragons, she forgot about Gateskin and concentrated on them instead, giving the King a chance to send more spells to stop her from harming the dragons.

Aharona, Navaeha and Jelitza could feel the heat coming from the black cloud and the tension that the dragons were exuding. They called out to their dragons' minds to find out what was happening.

Evander sent a message to Navaeha, "Don't worry, we have Elowen disarmed. She will not be a threat to anyone."

"Elowen is here?" Aharona cried out as she exchanged shocked expressions with her sister and cousin.

"What are we going to do to prevent her from destroying everyone and everything?" Navaeha asked.

"We must let our dragons take care of her. She does not like dragons and I think she is also a little fearful of them and their powers."

"Do you really think so?" Jelitza questioned in disbelief.

"Yes, I do. Don't you notice how she stays away from them and keeps a wide berth when we fly near her?"

"Wow, I never really thought about that, but you are right, Aharona," Jelitza exclaimed in shock.

"Do we need to do anything to help them, sister?" Navaeha asked, anxiously.

Aharona answered with a smirk, "No, let them take care of her. Gateskin is there too. With all the powers they have I think they can handle her."

"I sure hope so, Aharona," Navaeha said but didn't feel as certain.

The dust was swirling around so thick now and there was fire and smoke flying back and forth between the dragons and Elowen while Gateskin kept the fire from going toward the villagers.

The villagers looked up and became alarmed when they saw fire shooting back and forth across the sky. They were still unaware that a woman was amongst it all.

Gateskin kept the area from clearing too much to keep the people from seeing what was really happening.

Hotenfaran and Procelina lent their powers to back up the King along with their son, Arubane, who flew alongside them sending spells back and forth. Jenna and Henno were also in the mix to lend a hand which was weakening the stronghold that the Dark Fairy was sending their way.

CHAPTER FIFTY-EIGHT

Solinara was busy in her workshop when she felt the disturbance in the air. She could feel that Gateskin was in the middle of it.

She called out to her children and told them, "Stay inside. There is something happening at the search site. I must go there and find out if your father needs my help."

Serena spoke up first, "Let us go with you, Mother. We can all use our powers collectively to aid in whatever you need to do to help Father."

"Yes, please, Mother. You know how powerful we all are and more so together," Simon related in a serious tone.

"I am powerful too, Mother. Please let us go," Catalina said as she pleaded her case.

Solinara sighed heavily and finally said, "All right, follow me and stay behind me, please. I have no idea what we will encounter and I want you to be safe. Your father will not be pleased to see you there."

Serena smiled but concentrated to try and hear what was going on in the field as they flew closer.

"Mother, it's the dragons. They are back," Serena announced in excitement. "I can hear that they and Father are fighting something else. He and the dragons are working together. We must hurry."

"Yes, I am getting a message now from your father. He needs our help. Hurry!"

When they arrived at the scene all they could see was smoke and fire at first until it drifted away with a wave of their hands.

The Queen could see her husband, brother, and his wife and child along with Henno and Jenara assisting Gateskin with spells to stop Elowen.

Gateskin turned to see his family there and immediately pushed them behind him speaking to his wife in her mind,

"Keep the children behind you. Don't let them do anything to rile Elowen or she will harm them."

"Of course. I'm sorry I let them come with me. They convinced me that you would need them too."

"I know how they are. Don't worry. The dragons are keeping her busy. She may be a little tired. She can't keep this up much longer but the dragons can."

"They are amazing, aren't they, Gateskin?" Solinara articulated, in awe.

"Yes, I am impressed too. The sisters tell me that there are no limits to what powers they have. I've been thinking of acquiring one for Sovorotskina for protection."

"Really? Do you think we can obtain one from Dragonaria?"

"I will find out soon once this is over."

The children whispered back and forth. "Do you hear Father's thoughts?" Catalina gasped in surprise. "He wants to get a dragon."

"What?" Simon stated in shock. "Really? Did he say that?"

"I thought he did. Did you hear him say that to Mother, Serena?" Catalina inquired.

"You shouldn't be eave-dropping on our parent's conversation, Catalina. You know better than to do that."

"Sorry, Serena. I couldn't help myself."

"Ssh, be quiet. We will discuss this later." Serena was concentrating on watching the struggle back and forth and spotted Spindle coming her way.

"You shouldn't be here, Serena. None of you should, for that matter," Spindle exclaimed in alarm. "It's too dangerous for you. Let me escort you back home."

"No, I want to stay. I'm fine, Spindle. What is happening now? The smoke and fire are clearing. Is it over? Did Elowen give up?"

"No, but your father is speaking with her. I think he is trying to convince her to give up."

"Do you think she will?"

"I don't know, but I certainly hope so."

The three dragons drew in a deep breath and were ready to incinerate Elowen if she didn't stop when Gateskin flew in between Elowen and the dragons to stop them.

"This is over, Elowen. It's time for you to go home. There is nothing here for you. Once we find the Medallion, it will be destroyed."

"No, you can't destroy it! I will take it away from here. If you give it to me, I will leave and never come back, I promise."

"That will never happen, Elowen. Leave now or I will let the dragons take care of you forever."

She looked up at the Gateskin and then at the dragons who were breathing deeply, preparing to spit fire her way more seriously.

"All right. I will leave. But I will be back to see if you changed your mind about giving it to me."

"That is not going to happen, Elowen. I will not change my mind."

The dragons watched Elowen fly away and came back down to their mistresses who fussed over them, assuring that they were not injured.

Gateskin turned and thanked everyone for their help in curtailing the spells that

Elowen sent his way and sent them back to their homes for now.

He flew with his family to a safe place away from the smoke and dust.

"Gateskin, are you injured?" Solinara asked him as she touched his face that was darkened by the soot from the smoke and fire.

"No, I'm not. You need to take our children back home. There is nothing for them to do here. The dragons will continue their search and then I will be home later."

"Okay, but if you need me again, please call me right away this time. You could have called me and not have waited for me to come on my own."

"It wasn't necessary, Solinara. I did not want to put you in any danger."

The two sisters and cousin came forward to see Queen Solinara and the children.

"Hello again. Sorry to cause you any concern. Our dragons did have things in hand. We had no idea that Elowen was coming here today to cause any trouble."

"Yes, I see. It is not your fault. Thank you for bringing these magnificent creatures back to save us from your sister. We may not have been able to do this on our own."

"Our pleasure, Queen. We promise to be gone as soon as the Medallion is found and destroyed."

"It's all right. It was a thrill once again to see them, and this time in action. They are glorious!"

"Thank you, Queen. I think they are enjoying themselves. This is the first time they have been able to really let go with the smoke and fire."

Solinara whispered to Aharona, "Do you think that we could obtain one of these incredible creatures for our land?"

"I don't see why not. But I will have to speak to our father about that. That may take a little convincing on our part. He would want to come here to see where the dragon would be living."

"I think that can be arranged." Solinara nodded and spoke to Gateskin's mind.

***

Back on Dragonaria King Marcellinus and Queen Isla were pacing in anger and disappointment after hearing from Mianna about their three daughters' journey to Noella Province once again.

"Thank you, Mianna, for sharing this with us. We need to go there and put a stop to this once and for all. You should go back to your hut where it is safe. Don't let Elowen know what you did or harm could come to you."

"Yes, Queen. I plan to stay hidden away from her for a long time. I know that I was wrong to befriend and trust her. She is pure evil. I need to apologize to Aharona and Navaeha for not being a true friend anymore. I feel ashamed."

"I'm sure they will understand and forgive you, Mianna, in time," the Queen said with a sad expression.

"Thank you, Queen Isla. I hope they do one day."

Mianna moved away with her head low and shoulders slumped as she walked back home to hide from Elowen.

CHAPTER FIFTY-NINE

Gateskin became aware of his wife's thoughts and responded, "You didn't waste any time asking about adopting a dragon, Solinara?"

"No, I didn't. I thought it would be a perfect time to do that while they are here. If they left, we wouldn't be able to do that."

"Yes, that's true. What did Aharona say to that?" Gateskin asked, with curiosity.

"She must speak with her father. She will need to convince him that this is a good place for a dragon to live. She also insists that her father will want to visit with us to ensure that."

"Hmm, I see. That may not be a good idea after all, having more visitors here," Gateskin recommended.

"Yes, dear. You may be right. But how will we obtain a dragon if not that way. We cannot steal one," Solinara guffawed.

"Of course not. But we need to think about this a little longer. There are several conditions we have to meet in order to have a dragon here."

"Are you worried about feeding one, Gateskin?"

"Well, yes, that is one thing to think about. The other concerns are where to keep it and protect it from other lands and rulers who may want to steal, harm, or destroy it."

"Are you thinking about Kaposkaran?"

"Well, yes, especially him. But the other rulers would fear it and so would their people."

"You would have to inform all of them about the fact that we will be obtaining one here first. Then once we have one, we need to ensure that it is well fed and taken care of without fear for the safety of all our animals."

"You are correct on all aspects, Solinara."

"But you still sound hesitant about this. You need not worry about food. I will take care of that like I have with the wolves and Catlings."

"I believe you can handle the food issue, but what about the safety of our animals? We need to train the dragon to not eat any of them. How do we do that other than putting a spell on it that would wear off and have to be reapplied?"

Spindle hovered nearby and listened but stayed silent. He did not want to interrupt his King and Queen in their discussion.

"Well, that is something you will need to ask the sisters. They trained their own dragons and most likely can train one for us."

"Let's give this more thought, Solinara. In the meantime, we will keep searching for the Medallion."

The sisters watched as the King and Queen were in deep conversation. They shared their thoughts with each other too.

"Do you think that they are discussing getting a dragon?" Navaeha asked.

"Most likely they are. I don't know if Father will approve of this. He will be upset with us for coming here again without his approval. He may not even give us a chance to explain or ask about giving King Gateskin a dragon."

"The King is coming our way. Let's discuss this later. We need to get our dragons back to work on the search," Navaeha stated as she smiled at the King.

"Are they rested enough, Aharona?" Gateskin inquired.

Aharona nodded and replied, "Of course. They have rested for a while and are ready."

"Good. I would like to finish this tonight if we could. If not, you may not be able to come back. Your father may not allow you to do that once he finds out what you are doing here."

"Yes, I fear that he will not. Are you still interested in a dragon for Sovorotskina? We could use that as an excuse to come back."

"Do you think your father will allow this?" Gateskin asked as he waited for Aharona to mull this over.

"Who knows? We will try to convince him that is why we came back here and need to come back again to bring a dragon and stay long enough to train it for you."

"Oh, yes, I was going to ask that next. Can you train it not to eat any of our animals or people?" King Gateskin asked.

"Of course. That would have to be done. No one or anything would be safe here otherwise," Aharona confirmed.

"We would have to stay here until the dragon was completely trained and then instruct you on how to keep it that way," Navaeha continued the explanation.

"There is much that we do not know about dragons and need to learn," Gateskin stated.

"We would make sure you were well informed, King Gateskin. Let's get our dragons back to work. Okay?" Aharona suggested.

"Sure, let them do their magic," the King agreed.

Gateskin looked up at Spindle who had been quiet all this time. "What do you think about this dragon business, my good man?"

"Well, I am fascinated by them, King. I think it would be a good thing to have one, maybe more than one. One may get lonely."

"Yes, indeed, Spindle. You are right. One would get lonely," Gateskin chuckled at the thought.

CHAPTER SIXTY

Elowen arrived back on Dragonaria, disgruntled and ready to fight back again. She would not give up that easily.

She would find her father and let him know what her sisters and cousin were doing. That would put a stop to their search, giving her a chance to go back and find it herself. She snickered as she flew over to her father's castle.

When she arrived there her parents were pacing back and forth and looking upset. They must have found out that her sisters were gone again. She would step in now and cause more havoc for her siblings.

"Elowen, what brings you here?" her mother queried with a frown, already knowing where Elowen and her sisters had gone.

"I know you are not happy to see me, Mother, but I thought it was my duty as the oldest daughter to let you know what my younger siblings were doing."

"What are you trying to tell us, Elowen?" her father asked as his displeasure in seeing her was evident in his tone.

"Ahh, Father. It is good to see you too. I know it has been a long time," Elowen said with a smirk.

"What is it you want to share with us, daughter?" he pushed her to speak.

"Well, I think you should know where my sisters and cousin are at this moment."

"Spill it, Elowen, and stop playing games. We are not in the mood for your repartee," Marcellus blurted out in anger.

"Oh, Father, no need to lose your temper now. You know how tenuous your heart is. I wouldn't want you to tax yourself unnecessarily."

Isla put her arms around her husband and whispered, "Patience, dear. Take a deep breath. Let me handle Elowen."

Marcellus did as his wife suggested and nodded.

"Now, Elowen, tell us what this is all about and no more hesitation on your part. I know that you are dying to share what your sisters are doing so they will get into trouble. This is what you always did since you were all young. We know how you play these mind games and we are sick of them. I don't think you even have to tell us where your sisters are. We already know. They shared this with us before they left with our permission. So now you can return to your cabin on the other side of the island with your Dark Magic and leave us all alone."

"Mother, I am hurt. I was just trying to do my duty as a loving daughter and sister. Well, since you already know where they are then I will take my leave." Elowen flew away without another word.

"Why did you do that, Isla?"

"We don't know if they are in trouble."

"If they were in trouble, Elowen would have shared that gleefully, sad to say. We do know where they are, Marcellus, and where they have been before - Noella Province. We need to protect Mianna. Harm will surely come to her if Elowen finds out she was betrayed."

"Yes, I realize that too, dear. But we need to set boundaries for our daughters and niece to obey," the King stated firmly.

"They seem to be attracted to this place for whatever reason. They will come back and you will not say a word to them. Let them come to us and share whatever they need to share. This way they will not be afraid to share with us another time."

"Are you saying that we should not punish them for their disobedience?"

"Yes, that is what I am saying for the time being. Let them think they are not in trouble and they will want to share more with us that way."

"Is that like saying, give them honey instead of vinegar and they will keep coming back?"

"Yes, dear. That's it exactly. Let's go home and wait for them to come to us. I will make you a delicious supper."

"Now you are saying something that I like to hear."

"I know." Isla smiled and put her arm through her husband's as they went back inside their castle.

***

Elowen sat in her hut and stewed over what her mother had said. She didn't believe her for one minute that she knew where her sisters were. "Mother had played a trick on me and turned the tide this time. Next time I will be smarter and think of something else to rein them in," she mused.

She turned to her bench where she had laid out her potions and began to put together a stronger one for when she would return to Noella Province. This time she wouldn't return home empty-handed.

CHAPTER SIXTY-ONE

The people of Votovia and the other lands were frightened. They had seen a black cloud flying over Noella Province. They feared it might be Wizards from Parotovina coming back to destroy their lands and take their offspring as they did over one hundred years ago.

A few of the men went to visit King Cavelan to report what they had seen.

The King was sitting in his conference room when they were ushered in by his guards.

"What is the problem?" he asked as he saw the troubled expressions on the men's faces.

"Sorry to bother you, King Cavelan. But we thought it was urgent that you know about what we saw."

***

While this was going on in Votovia, similar meetings were taking place in Merona, Merlina and Amora where villagers were going to their own king's castle to report what they saw.

In Merona, which was in the center of the province, several men and women gathered outside the castle of The Healers waiting to speak with them.

In Merlina, the village next to Parotovina, King Zuri greeted some of his people to hear what they had to say about a black cloud and fire they had seen in the sky over Sovorotskina.

In Amora, which was in the farthest tip of the province, discussions were going on like the other villages of black clouds, fire shooting across the sky, and smoke that drifted far and wide.

The leaders of the lands called each other from their conference rooms, opening the Channel Spell that King Gateskin had created for them to keep in touch with him. They waited for Gateskin to appear in his window to report to him what their people had said.

Gateskin wasn't in his conference room but still leading the search for the Medallion unaware of the other rulers' concern over what he was doing.

***

The dragons were searching further up Mt. Ailylene now as the dust kept floating up and around, dropping these particles that were now on everyone below.

Gateskin put his hands out and collected some of this dust and realized what it was - silver. They had hit a pocket of silver. He spread word to his people to collect the silver dust and put it into bags.

The villagers eagerly did this knowing now how valuable it was. They whispered amongst each other as they swept the dust into piles and pushed it into bags, stacking them along the border of the trees as they waited for further instructions from their King.

The three dragons worked together to keep digging one vein of silver and pulled out a large piece of it after blowing on it to solidify and cool it a little. They brought it over to the King for his inspection.

Gateskin waited until it completely cooled before touching it and nodded to the dragons in thanks. They went back to pulling more of the silver out of the mountain and laid each piece at the feet of the King.

The sisters and cousin hurried over to inspect the silver and were in awe of its beauty. They had never seen so much silver in one place. They helped

Gateskin pick it up and place it into a bag and stack it next to the other bags.

Soon there were many more bags filled as the villages kept bringing in more bags from their homes to accommodate the metal.

Everyone was so enthralled with the silver that they did not notice the dragons had stopped drilling with fire and had flown down into the hole they had just made to look closer at something that was down there.

Verite went in first since she was the smallest and could fit in the hole easily. As she backed out of the hole the other dragons followed her.

Gateskin looked up to see the dragons flying down to land at his feet. Verite had something in her claws and placed it at the King's feet.

"What is it, King?" Aharona asked, anxiously.

"Is it the Medallion?" Navaeha probed.

"Can I see it?" Jelitza queried.

"Let me look at it. Please be patient everyone," King Gateskin pleaded.

Gateskin picked it up carefully after making sure it was not hot to touch before studying the metal box.

CHAPTER SIXTY-TWO

The rulers of the other lands were still waiting to reach Gateskin to share their concerns. When Gateskin did not appear after an hour, they spoke to one another and finally decided to send one of them to inspect the land of

Sovorotskina to ensure that the King and his people were not in some kind of trouble.

King Votovia was voted to be the one to venture there since he and Gateskin were good friends and had worked together in the past to rescue the Taken Ones. He also lived the closest in proximity to Sovorotskina.

King Votovia agreed and enlisted several of his best men to accompany him with weapons in case they needed to defend themselves and Sovorotskina.

Even though the King could fly, the rest of the men could not. They would therefore all fly there with the help of a spell that was cast by Votovian Wizards to make haste their travels.

***

Back in Sovorotskina Gateskin told all the people to return to their homes and that he would report the findings to them the next day after inspecting the box. The people acquiesced since they were tired and welcomed returning home to their families for a hearty supper and a soft bed.

The three dragons were exhausted from their efforts too and lay down to rest. Gateskin stepped closer to them and told them, "I am pleased and thankful for your efforts to uncover not only the silver but this box. I hope it will be what I expect it to be. I can't thank you enough, but I can supply you with a hearty meal and some water before you sleep."

Out of thin air the King pulled six furry creatures and handed two to each dragon who quickly gulped them down and burped loudly with pleasure. He also placed large bowls of water at the dragons' feet which they quickly slurped at nosily.

The dragons bowed in thanks to the King and sighed happily.

The sisters and cousin giggled over their dragons' behavior and whispered to them, "You must rest now and do not venture from here. We will return shortly and fly home."

The dragons nodded sleepily, lay down under their protective camouflage, and were soon snoring loudly as they continued to burp and hiccup as they digested their furry meals.

The three women followed close behind Gateskin, anxious to see what their dragons had found. They did not say a word for the King was deep in thought and looking down at the box as they walked along.

When they arrived at the King's home, the Queen was there to greet them. She had prepared a large meat pie that was steaming on the stove with two loaves of bread and butter on the table.

The children were setting the table and looked up at them in surprise when they saw their father was holding a box in his hands.

"Did you find the Medallion, Father?" Serena asked as she rushed forward to peek at it.

Simon and Catalina were right behind her and trying to look over her shoulder.

"Please let us inside, children. I will share what was found soon enough. Now it is time to get washed up and eat. We are all hungry and tired and our visitors want to return home soon."

"Yes, Father. Sorry," Serena said as she moved aside to allow everyone to come in.

Gateskin met his wife's eyes and sent a message to her. "I think it is what we were looking for. It has some strange engravings on it. I will have our Wizards examine it before I attempt to open it. It may have a spell on it that can harm whoever tries to break the seal."

"Yes, I agree. Keep the children away from it."

"Of course. I will put it in my conference room under lock and key until after we eat."

"Good idea, dear. Get cleaned up and eat. You will feel better and ready to inspect it."

Serena watched her parents as they discussed the box. She did not enter their conversation even though she could have but her parents would know that she did and would not be pleased with her. She sighed and tried to be patient. She knew that her father would share what the find was soon.

Simon looked at Serena and shared his thoughts with her, "Do you know what it is, Serena? What did our parents say just now?"

"I can't enter their thoughts, Simon. You know that."

"Okay. I won't push it. I understand. I wish I could do that."

"Do you know what it is, Serena?" Catalina entered their thoughts.

"No, but I suspect it is the Medallion and soon we will know when Father opens the box."

"It's like a birthday present. It's so exciting to open one but more exciting to wonder what is in the box."

"I agree, Catalina," Serena chuckled.

"Hmm, I wonder," Simon responded.

"No, you will not go near it, Simon. Get that out of your head right now. Father will be extremely angry with you." Serena met her brother's eyes with a stern expression of warning. "Besides, it could be dangerous."

"Okay, I understand. Please don't burn me with those eyes, Serena."

CHAPTER SIXTY-THREE

As Gateskin locked the box in his safe in the conference room he noticed the Channel Spell had been opened. He touched the air that was vibrating and waited to see if anyone was trying to reach him.

The Healers of Merona appeared in the window along with King Noderan of Amora and King Zuri of Merlina.

"What's going on, everyone? Were you trying to reach me?"

The Healers were the first to respond, "Yes, we were waiting patiently for you to answer the summons. Are you in any trouble there?"

"Trouble? Why do you ask?"

King Noderan of Amora answered with a sigh, "Well, our people in each land came to seek our help. They saw fire in the sky and smoke and a black cloud going toward your land."

"A black cloud, you say."

"Yes, and fire and smoke. My people were quite alarmed and worried for your people. They suspected that you were all in danger," King Zuri answered with concern. "In fact, King Cavelan and his men are on their way to your village to aid you in any way that you need."

"There is no need for concern. I will meet with Cavelan and reassure him that all is well. I planned to contact you all again about the search that I am doing now. I think you were already aware of the Medallion that is buried somewhere in Sovorotskina and my search."

"Yes, I remember you mentioning that recently. Is there a problem with that? Did you find it?" The Healers asked, with interest.

"I thought that was just a myth, Gateskin," King Noderan added.

"Well, that I will know soon. I promise to apprise you of the results of our search."

"Is that what caused the smoke and fire in the sky?" King Zuri inquired.

"Yes, it was. I should explain a little to you. I used three dragons from Dragonaria to assist in the search. They used fire to dig and uncover the earth more efficiently than I or my men could do."

"That is interesting. Dragons did that?" The Healers were fascinated and wanted to hear more about these creatures.

"Yes, it was amazing to watch these magnificent creatures in action. They worked tirelessly and never complained."

"It must have been quite a sight to witness," King Noderan stated in awe.

"It was, Noderan. It was something that I never would have seen if I hadn't used them in this way with the consent of their mistresses, three women from Dragonaria."

"These are the same visitors that came before with their dragons?" King Noderan asked.

"Yes. Their young cousin joined them this time to assist in the search."

"I see. Did you find it?" King Zuri asked.

"Well, I did find something. I am not sure what it is yet. I need to confer with my Wizards who can decipher the inscriptions and designs on the box."

"You found a box? What kind of box?" The Healers asked.

"It is a box of some kind of metal. I have locked it up for safety. I fear there is Dark Magic in it and will not open it until I know that it is not dangerous to anyone."

"I see. I agree that it could contain Dark Magic, Gateskin. You better be careful," King Noderan recommended.

"I plan to be careful, Noderan. I assure you."

"About the black cloud, Gateskin, what was that?" King Zuri probed.

"Well, that was a woman named Elowen who lives on Dragonaria that I mentioned to you. She is the eldest sister of the other women who came. Elowen practices Dark Magic. What your people saw was her black cloak flying over our province."

"I don't like the sound of that, Gateskin. Is she still around?" The Healers asked, anxiously.

"No, I told her to leave and she did. I do believe that she will be back, for she wants the Medallion for herself."

"You cannot let her have it, Gateskin," King Noderan stated with vehemence.

"I know. I will do all I can to keep her from taking it. I may need your help. Will you support me in this endeavor?"

"Of course. We will do all we possibly can with the help of our Wizards," King Zuri added as he looked at the other rulers as they nodded in agreement.

"Thank you. I appreciate your assistance. This is going to be a difficult thing to handle on my own. I promise to contact you as soon as I know what is in the box and if it is safe."

"We look forward to hearing from you on this matter. Don't we?" King Noderan responded and waited for his fellow rulers to nod once again.

"Good! I'm relieved to see you are all in agreement. I know how difficult this will be to keep secrets from your people. I don't want anyone to get alarmed."

"We will do our best to keep this quiet. I'm sure Cavelan will be interested to hear this too. He should be there shortly," The Healers added.

"Thank you again. We will talk soon." King Gateskin ended the conference call and joined his family once again.

CHAPTER SIXTY-FOUR

There was a knock at the door as Gateskin, his family, and the three women from Dragonaria were finishing up their supper. He left the table to open the door to his new visitors.

"Gateskin, are you all right?" King Cavelan asked as he looked his friend over.

"Of course, Cavelan. Come in, my friend, and have some refreshments. Bring your men in too. You have traveled a long time."

"It really isn't long since we flew as quickly as we could to rescue you."

"Rescue me? Did you fear that I was in trouble?" Gateskin responded with a grin.

"Well, are you not?"

"No, we all are fine. Let me explain."

Gateskin relayed what he had done with the search, who assisted him and what caused the fire, smoke, and black cloud. He also told of his conference call with the other rulers and their mutual concern.

"We were all worried about you and your people. We feared the worst when my people saw the fire and smoke."

"We are all well, I assure you. We did find a box that the dragons managed to uncover along with a vein of silver."

"A box and silver? Where did you find these?"

"Inside Mt. Ailylene. We would not have been able to find it if it wasn't for the tenacity and hard work of the dragons. They are magnificent creatures and well behaved."

"Hmm, interesting. I would have loved to see them in action with all the fire and smoke. Didn't this frighten your people?"

"A little at first but then they were in awe of the majesty of these dragons."

"I can only imagine what that was like," King Cavelan said in wonder. "Maybe one day I will see one."

"I believe that is possible sooner than you think."

"Really?"

"Let me introduce you to the mistresses of these marvelous dragons. This is Aharona, Navaeha and their cousin, Jelitza. They were getting ready to return home now. I will lead the way to the dragons who are resting after their strenuous task."

"Should I bring my men with me?"

"You will not need protection, Cavelan. But you will need to let your men know what they will be seeing and that these creatures are not dangerous to any of us. These women have complete control over them."

Cavelan quickly explained to his men where they were going after they finished their refreshments. He watched their eyes grow large at the thought of seeing dragons for the first time.

"No worries, men. Stay close to me and King Gateskin. No need to defend me. The King assured me that they are not dangerous to us as long as their mistresses are here to command them to behave."

King Cavelan's men nodded in disbelief but followed closely behind him, King Gateskin and the three women. They whispered amongst themselves and looked around them for any sign of trouble.

When they reached the dragons, the three women stepped forward and tapped their charges on their noses to awaken them. They whispered into their large ears to behave for they had visitors who wanted to meet them.

Callum rose up and bowed to the visitors and winked at King Gateskin to reassure him that they were safe.

Evander lifted his huge silver wings to show them off and intimidate the people standing there who wore frightened expressions and backed away in fear. He grumbled and snorted, sending smoke out of his nostrils, clearly pleased with himself.

Navaeha tapped Evander on his nose in warning and the dragon lay down and closed his eyes, visibly disgruntled.

Verite, the smallest and only female dragon, bowed and smiled at the people, trying to make them relax.

King Cavelan and his men were all holding their breaths as they gazed at these colorful creatures that glowed in the moonlight.

Cavelan released his breath and said, "This is an extreme pleasure to meet you all. I feel such a wonder just looking at your magnificence. I am honored and humbled. Thank you for this unexpected thrill."

His men mumbled their thanks and stepped back, not quite sure if they were safe to be so close to these enormous creatures.

Callum spoke up, much to the surprise of the visitors, "We are humbled that you feel that way, King. I feel that you are a king in the way you handle yourself. Am I right?"

King Cavelan nodded, speechless to hear that a dragon could talk.

"It is quite a shock, isn't it, Cavelan, to hear a dragon speak like that?" King Gateskin stated, with a smile.

"Yes, I was speechless and could only respond with a nod to him."

"I know how you feel. I felt the same way when I first met them. Wouldn't it be quite an honor to have one on our lands?" King Gateskin suggested.

"Yes, I was just thinking about that myself. Is that at all possible?" King Cavelan agreed.

King Gateskin looked at the three women and waited for them to respond.

Aharona nodded and said, "Yes, it is quite possible, but we must get permission from our father before we can go ahead and train one for you."

"That is incredible to think about, Gateskin. Are you going to get one?" King Cavelan asked, in eager anticipation.

"Maybe. We are not sure yet. Solinara would love one to help protect our village and all the province."

"Yes, I can see how that would be wonderful."

Aharona cleared her throat to get King Gateskin's attention. "Sorry to bother you, King Gateskin, but we must leave at once. It is getting later than I wanted to leave. Our parents will be looking for us."

"Of course. Let me put a spell on you and your dragons to send you home swiftly and safely under cover."

"Thank you. It was our pleasure to help you. We will contact you soon if our father approves of the dragon transfer here. We can't promise anything though, for he will be upset with us once again."

"I understand. If you need me all you have to do is call out my name even in a whisper and say, 'help.' I will send a spell to bring you back here undercover once again."

"Okay. We will do that, King. Thank you."

Navaeha added, "We would love to know what is in the box whenever you open it."

"Of course I will let you know. I will also keep an eye out for your sister, Elowen's return. I suspect she will be back."

"I think she will. Sorry for any trouble she caused or will cause you in the future, King Gateskin," Aharona stated.

"It is not your fault that she is what she is. Do not worry about her. I will handle whatever she sends our way."

"Goodbye and thank you for your kindness and hospitality. Nice to meet you, King Cavelan and your men."

King Cavelan bowed and his men nodded as they watched the colorful, glorious creatures fly away.

"Come back to my home, Cavelan, and we can discuss this in more detail."

"Men, follow us," King Cavelan commanded his men who were still staring at the disappearing dragons.

CHAPTER SIXTY-FIVE

The two Quintaroons were getting restless and wanted to leave their huts. They were unaware of one another being so close but the first Quintaroon, Quintal, now knew about the existence of another Quintaroon from the King.

He also now realized why the scent was familiar in the area. He wanted to search for the smell that kept drifting his way.

Taron the second Quintaroon felt something in the air too and wanted to find it. He tried once again to step out of his hut but his foot wouldn't leave the threshold. He kept doing this again and again and soon grew tired of it. He looked around the hut and checked the windows. He tried to open each one, but to no avail. He went into the room that was for his toilet but did not find a way out there either.

Unbeknownst to either of the Quintaroons, they did not know two very important things, that they were sensitive to water which would make them disappear or that they could shrink or grow if they ate people.

There were also weaknesses in their makeup. They were afraid of the dark, blinded by bright lights, and fearful of rodents and allergic to nuts.

Quintal sat down to have a drink and a snack that was left for him by the King. He sipped the juice and ate the biscuits that the Queen had made and sighed. This may be a boring life but at least no one was trying to kill him. It would be perfect if only he could go outside and get some fresh air every day.

Taron was doing the same thing in his hut - eating and drinking what was left for him by King Gateskin. He lifted his nose every so often to sniff the air. There was something out there. Was it possible that there were more like him? He wondered.

***

Serena and her siblings were taking a walk around their property and passed by the huts of both Quintaroons which were located on either side of the King's house. The children felt a disturbance as they got nearer to the Quintaroons.

Simon looked up at the window of Quintal's hut and saw him looking back at him beckoning him forward. "Is that the Quintaroon, Serena?"

"Yes, it is. He is now a man though. But Father did say to stay away from him and do not open his door or that of the second Quintaroon, Taron."

"Why can't we go visit with them if they are now men and safe?" Catalina asked.

"Father isn't too sure if they could change again and doesn't want them to escape if we opened their doors."

"Can I go up to the window and talk to Quintal?" Simon queried.

"No, let's go check on the animals. Father is in conference now and wants us to ensure that they are all fed and doing well."

"All right, Serena. I wish I could be boss occasionally too," Simon expressed his exasperation.

Catalina waved at Quintal and then as they passed Taron's hut did the same to him.

"They both look so sad, Serena. I think they need us to visit them. I would not like being locked up inside every day."

"I know, Catalina. But we must listen to Father. He knows them better than we do. He is only concerned for our safety."

"Okay. Can I feed the chickens this time, Serena?" Catalina asked, already forgetting about the Quintaroons.

"Sure, but don't overfeed them. Check to see if Milly needs milking and brush and feed Hank, the horse, too. Simon will help you. I need to take care of the wolves."

"Wait until we finish here, Serena. We want to help with the wolves. I want to see if there are any more cubs. Right, Simon?" Catalina expressed her excitement.

"Hurry up and you will get to help me. There are plenty to feed. I'll be inside Mother's workshop getting more of the food. You can come there and help carry some of the food out."

Simon led his youngest sister to the barn and gave her orders. "Who made you my boss, Simon?" Catalina exclaimed, perturbed, and declining to obey.

"Well, I am older than you so that makes me the boss. Father would agree."

"Who said he would?" Catalina voiced her feistiness.

"Stop complaining and hurry up so we can go see the wolves," Simon stated, but stopped talking when he saw his sister's face blanch as she stared at something behind him.

CHAPTER SIXTY-SIX

Gateskin and Cavelan were deep in conversation when they heard Catalina's screams.

They jumped up and ran with Cavelan's men following close behind them.

Solinara had heard her daughter's distressed call and was already running toward the direction of the scream.

When they all arrived at the barn all they saw were the animals who were eating their feed. Nothing seemed to be disturbed.

Serena came out of the workshop and hurried over to join them. "Where are Catalina and Simon? I left them here to feed the animals. Who screamed?"

"It was Catalina. I would recognize her scream anywhere," Solinara exclaimed in alarm. "Where are they? That is what I want to know, and what happened to make her scream?"

Gateskin waved his hand at his wife and beckoned her forward. "Go to Quintal's hut to make sure he is still there. I will check on Taron. If they got out, they could have frightened the children."

The Queen raced over to Quintal's hut and knocked on the door. Quintal opened it up so quickly that Solinara backed away in alarm.

"Sorry to frighten you, Queen Solinara. I was at the door and trying to open it to go for a walk. Did you come to let me out?"

"No, Quintal. I was just checking on you to see if you needed anything."

"Well, I don't need anything but would love to go outside for a walk. Will you go with me?"

"Sorry, Quintal. I will have the King come get you soon. I must find my children."

"Are they lost? I just saw them walk by here recently. Can I do anything to help?"

"No. It's okay. Go rest."

"I am all rested. Let me help you find them. I can fly around if I can turn back into a Quintaroon."

"That is not a good idea, Quintal. It is not safe for you to do that."

"I can learn to control it if you help me," Quintal pleaded.

"I'll check with the King. Stay put for now. Thank you for offering your help though."

Quintal sighed and closed the door and sulked as he looked out the window and watched the Queen walk away. He also noticed the King and some other men wandering around. He wondered what was happening out there. If only he could get outside and help them.

Gateskin was at Taron's door at this time and got the same response from him.

"Hello, King Gateskin. It's so good to see you. Can I go outside for a walk now? I am getting so tired of being confined here."

"Not now, Taron. Maybe later. I need to find my children."

"Are they lost? I just saw them pass by here a little while ago. Your little one is sweet. She waved at me."

"Thank you. Yes, they are lost. We heard Catalina, the sweet one, scream and worry that she may be injured."

"Yes, I heard that too but I thought they were just playing. Can I help you find her?"

"No, Taron. Thank you though. I will come back later to bring you for a walk. Okay?"

"All right. I look forward to it. If I can be of assistance, please let me know. You have been so kind to let me stay here."

Gateskin nodded and walked away to join his wife, King Cavelan, and his men who all shook their heads that they hadn't found the children either.

They were unaware that above their heads the children struggled for they were being held captive.

CHAPTER SIXTY-SEVEN

Spindle watched from his treetop as the black cloud returned to Sovorotskina. He knew she was nothing but trouble. He would keep an eye on her and report anything she did to the King.

The Sprite became alarmed when he saw the black cloud disappear inside the barn where the children were. He followed closely. He whispered to the children as he hovered close, "Don't worry I am here." Spindle flew to alert Gateskin about Elowen's return.

"Be quiet, both of you. I need to think this through. Who are you talking to?"

"We are just talking to each other. Why are you doing this to us, Elowen?" Simon asked.

"How do you know me?"

"We saw you during the search. Father didn't know we were watching from a distance. You are not a nice person," Catalina said in a strong voice.

"We are not afraid of you. Father will not be pleased that you took us like this," Simon stated, firmly, being the older sibling.

"I said be quiet. I need to think this through. Did your father find the Medallion?"

"I…don't know. Why do you want it?" Simon queried, frowning warily.

"None of your business what I want to do with it. Answer me. Did he find it?"

"We…are not supposed to say," Catalina stated and closed her mouth tightly when her brother gave her a look of warning.

"So that means that he did. I knew it. I listened to my sisters talk to my parents. I figured that they must have helped him find it before they returned home," Elowen said with a grin of pleasure. "Now all I need to do is get it from him. He will give it to me if he wants his children back."

"He will not give it to you, Elowen," Simon stated, with a grin that wavered.

"Don't be too sure about that, children. If he loves you more than life, he will."

Elowen flew down in front of the group but held the children close to her, wrapping her cloak around them.

Spindle stayed by Gateskin's side in case he was needed.

Queen Solinara screamed to Gateskin. "Get them away from her, please!" Turning to Elowen she stated, firmly, "You will not harm them, Elowen!"

"Elowen, I was expecting you. You do not need to take our children. We can discuss this right here. Let them go," King Gateskin commanded.

"No, I will not give them back unless you give me the Medallion."

"I do not have it, Elowen. What makes you think I do?"

"I heard my sisters arguing with my parents about helping you find it. They are in deep trouble and will not come back here. My parents forbid it," she lied.

"Sorry to hear that. But I will give you something else that we found instead."

"What? You found something else? What is it? Is it valuable?" Elowen's curiosity was piqued.

"Yes, it is."

"Well, is it as valuable as the Medallion?"

"Maybe more."

"Show me what it is and I will decide whether it is worth giving your children back."

"You will not harm them, Elowen or I will…" Queen Solinara did not finish her words when Gateskin touched her arm to calm her.

The children kept struggling to get out of Elowen's grip as she spoke to King Gateskin.

Spindle whispered to the Queen, "What about getting Quintal to help?" Solinara nodded to Spindle, stepped away and ran over to Quintal's hut and opened the door. "Will you still help us get our children?"

"Yes, I promise to help you. Where do you want me to look?"

"We know where they are, Quintal. We just need you to fly and pull them away from the grip of a Wizard who uses Dark Magic."

"Dark Magic?"

"I do not know how to stop Dark Magic but I will try to get the children away from her. All I have to do is change into a Quintaroon. Can you help me do that?"

Solinara thought for a moment and finally remembered what could be done. “Listen to me, Quintal. Get a drink of water quickly.”

“But I am not thirsty, Queen.”

“Yes, you are. Drink one now. It is the only way.”

Quintal went into his kitchen and poured himself a drink.

Solinara explained, as he drank, what would happen to him. “Follow me, Quintal. No one can see you. Now you will be able to help us.”

Quintal, now invisible much to his surprise, followed close behind the Queen until she stood next to a woman all in black holding two children.

He whispered to the Queen, “I see your children. What do you want me to do?”

Solinara whispered back to him, "Pull the children away from her and do not let her touch you."

"I will do my best, Queen."

The children were listening to their mother's thoughts, as well as Gateskin, as she explained to them what was about to happen.

Simon and Catalina nodded and put their hands out in front of them and waited to feel someone pulling them out of the arms of Elowen.

Quintal grabbed the children's outstretched hands and pulled them quickly away. Serena pushed her siblings toward home after meeting her parent's eyes. Quintal stepped away himself to stand next to the Queen waiting for further instructions.

Elowen yelled, "What? How did you do that?"

"You have no way to bargain now, Elowen. It is time you give up and return home never to come back here again," King Gateskin said with authority.

Once the children were free, they flew away from Elowen and back to their home to safety as instructed by their mother.

King Gateskin smiled at his wife as he watched his children fly away. He whispered, "Quintal, if you are there, come closer to me. Thank you for your help."

Elowen stood there not wanting to move. She knew something wasn't right but couldn't explain it.

Spindle watched and guffawed as Quintal saved the children much to the dismay of Elowen who looked thoroughly confused.

***

While this was going on Taron was watching from his window. He knocked to get someone's attention but they were all too busy with Elowen, all but Quintal who was still invisible.

Quintal moved toward the window and knocked back at Taron. He called out, "Who are you?"

CHAPTER SIXTY-EIGHT

Gateskin pooled his powers with Solinara and Cavelan and put a spell on Elowen to push her away from Noella Province and send her back to Dragonaria.

Hotenfaran, Procelina and Arubane, who came along to help, added their own powers to the mix as Solinara nodded her thanks to them, concentrating her efforts on disabling Elowen.

Elowen was powerless to do anything since all these powerful Wizards and Fairies together overtook her own powers and forced her to flee for her life.

The group cheered as they watched Elowen floundering in the sky trying to fly right-side up. Their spells had caused her to fly upside down all the way home.

Gateskin and Solinara hurried back home to see their children who were relating their adventure to Serena who had followed them back there. She listened and let them explain it all in detail.

When their parents entered the house, they rushed into their arms and cried in relief but wanted to know where Quintal was so they could thank him.

Hotenfaran and his wife and son stood aside until they were needed but spoke up and said, "We can go check on the Quintaroons, if you need our help."

Solinara gasped and looked at Gateskin as she cried out in alarm, "He is still out there and invisible."

King Gateskin told his brother-in-law and wife to stay with his family to protect them in case Quintal came there.

Gateskin flew back to find him. He looked everywhere until he saw Taron at his door talking to thin air.

"Taron, who are you speaking to?"

"Oh, King. I have a new friend, Quintal. He said he is a Quintaroon or used to be one just like me. I didn't know there was another one around. I am so happy to have a friend who I can talk to who will understand how I feel. He even told me that he became invisible after drinking water. Isn't that something?"

"Listen, the two of you. You cannot stay out here. Quintal, you must return to your hut."

"But, King, why can't I stay here with Taron. We can be roommates. That way we won't be so lonely all the time."

"Hmm, I think that could be arranged. Let me get some men so we can put your two cabins close together and connect them so you can still have your own space and time to spend together. Will that work for you?"

"That sounds perfect, doesn't it, Taron?"

"Oh, yes, that is perfect!"

"You can stay here, Quintal, until we can do this. Your invisibility will fade soon. It only lasts for a limited time. We still don't know how long though. It all depends upon how much water you drank. That is why I haven't given you water, only other drinks."

Quintal stepped inside and soon was back to himself as he shook hands with Taron and patted him on the back, happy to have found a fellow Quintaroon.

The two were so busy talking that they did not notice that the King had left them with the spell that would keep them inside until he came back.

When Gateskin returned home Solinara was waiting to hear what he had done to get Quintal back inside his hut.

The King explained what transpired and how happy the two men were now that they had each other to keep them from getting lonely and bored.

"You did not tell them anything else about their powers or weaknesses, Gateskin, did you?"

"No, but it won't be long before they discover them. Quintal and Taron both know that they can fly if they are in their Quintaroon states, and now that it may be possible in their present state to do that also."

"Yes, I remember that, dear," Solinara sighed.

"I am happy to see them together, Father," Catalina said with a wide smile. "They always look so sad as I walk by there. I wave at them to cheer them up. I wouldn't want to be alone all the time and never leave my room like they do. Can't you let them go outside a little every day together. We can walk with them to make sure they behave."

"That might be a good idea, Catalina. You are not only sweet like Quintal said, but also smart," her father said, with a grin.

"Quintal called me sweet? That's nice of him. I like him too," Catalina snickered.

"We will arrange something for you to do each day with them. You and Simon will do it together," Gateskin stated.

"Okay. That sounds like fun. We will get to know the Quintaroons better while we watch over them."

Solinara looked at her husband. "Are you sure they are safe with these men? What if they turn back into Quintaroons?"

"I don't think they will. They like being men and having some power even if they don't change. I didn't know if invisibility would work in their human form. How did you know that, Solinara?"

"Spindle suggested that I get Quintal to help. I didn't really know if he would become invisible. I took a chance to save our children. I told him that he would become invisible if he drank the water and he did."

"Did you put a spell on him, Mother?" Serena asked as she smiled at Spindle for his suggestion.

"No, I didn't have to. I had thought about that though. My only concern was saving you two." Turning to her two youngest children she hugged them and kissed their heads, thankful that they were unharmed.

"We are fine, Mother," Simon explained.

"She did not hurt us," Catalina said with a smile.

"I'm happy to hear that. If anything had happened to either of you, I..." Solinara choked up and sniffed away the tears.

"Don't cry, Mother. We love you. We were planning to do something ourselves, right Simon?"

Simon smiled and nodded, "We were working on a spell to free ourselves when Quintal pulled us away."

"I should have known," Gateskin chuckled.

"Do you think that Elowen will come back, Father?" Serena asked with concern.

"She probably will one day. But we will be ready for her."

"Yes, we will, Father!" Catalina piped up loud and clear.

A howling was heard from the wolves that startled everyone from their reverie.

CHAPTER SIXTY-NINE

Serena raced out to see what was upsetting the wolves. Everyone else was close behind her. Spindle was flying above her head to ensure that she was not harmed.

Cantok stepped forward and spoke to Serena, "We were just hungry, that is all. Sorry to startle you. We know that something bad was happening. Are the children safe now?"

"Yes, Cantok. Thank you for asking," Serena responded. "I was on my way to feed you when all this happened with my siblings. I will get your food. Please forgive me."

"No worries, Serena. We understand how important children are. More important than wolves."

"You are important to us, Cantok. All the wolves are like our family."

Serena ran over to the workshop and returned with a large dish of food for the wolves.

Cantok bowed to Serena in thanks and pulled some of the food out of the dishes to bring to his new cubs and mate.

Serena stayed there until all the wolves were fed and then went back into the house.

Spindle followed Serena until she was safely back inside before leaving. But Serena blew him a kiss in thanks before closing the door.

"Are they okay, Serena?" Solinara asked.

"Yes, they were just hungry. It was my fault. I didn't feed them before all this happened. Cantok was concerned about his new cubs."

"Oh, I see. I know how young ones can't wait to eat. I had three hungry and impatient ones myself," Serena giggled as she looked at her children.

King Cavelan and his men were outside waiting to say goodbye to King Gateskin when he came out to get his men to help move the two huts together for the Quintaroons.

"Sorry to keep you waiting here. Do you want to stay for supper? We have plenty left."

"No, things are all settled here. It's time we return. It might be a good idea to let the other rulers know what transpired so that they don't send some more men this way to rescue you. They may have seen the black cloud again."

"Right. I will do that right away, Cavelan. I might have forgotten. Thanks for your support."

"We were happy to be of assistance even if we didn't do anything."

"You did help get rid of Elowen for the time being until she returns."

"Hopefully she won't. Please let me know if you need me again, Gateskin. Also, I would love to hear what's in the box you discovered."

"Yes, I will contact you. But in the meantime, please take this as a token of thanks." Gateskin pulled out a large piece of silver out of his pocket and handed it to Cavelan.

"This is silver? Wow, it is beautiful, Gateskin! It has value?"

"Yes, it does. It can be melted down to make weapons, utensils, pans, or other things that would be useful to us."

"Thank you. I will give it to my Wizards to work on its properties and uses."

"I plan to do that too, Cavelan. They need to be kept busy. Right now, they will be working on the box."

"Take care, my friend. Talk to you soon, I hope, about the box."

"Yes, we will. Safe travels home."

The Kings bowed to one another and went their separate ways.

***

Back in Dragonaria, Elowen was tending her wounds, physical and emotional. She was quite upset about failing to obtain the Medallion a second time. There would be another day.

She spoke with her friend Mianna who was waiting for her return from Noella Province to hear about her adventure. Mianna feigned her disappointment to hear that it was not successful. She planned to keep an eye on Elowen while watching her own back as the King and Queen suggested.

The two sisters and cousin were nursing their own wounds after being punished by their parents even though they were not scolded as such but given the silent treatment which could be worse.

They had shared their travels and adventures with their parents without any repercussions. This kept them cautious for they did not know what their parents would do to them further.

***

In Parotovina, King Kaposkaran was cooking up a scheme once he heard about the search for the Medallion. He wanted it for himself. He listened to his men relating what they had heard throughout the villages about the search and the dragons who uncovered it inside Mt. Ailylene.

He would keep an eye out for the return of the dragons and this time he would stop them and take them for his own land. He knew that they were powerful and formidable creatures if he could control them.

He would also send out more men to spy in Sovorotskina to find out the latest news about the Medallion and its powers. He would stop at nothing to obtain that too.

CHAPTER SEVENTY

In Sovorotskina Gateskin's Wizards worked on the box deciphering its lettering and symbols and whether it was safe to open.

Gateskin listened to what they had discovered so far and was hesitant to let them open it. He did not want any of the Dark Magic to escape and harm his family and people.

***

Spindle flew over to see if he was needed in any way. He felt useless if he wasn't busy helping the King and his family. He stayed close by as always if needed.

"King Gateskin, I don't want to get in your way but I am here if you need me."

"Thank you, Spindle, for what you did the other day suggesting the Queen get Quintal to help. Did you know that he can turn invisible too?"

"Yes, I remembered what you told me about their strengths and weaknesses. I wasn't sure it would work but the Queen could always put a spell on him to make it work. That is what I thought would happen. I was surprised that she didn't have to do that."

"Yes, I was too. I don't know if I thanked you enough for watching over my children too. Simon and Catalina told me you were there to keep them company when they were being held captive by Elowen."

"It is my pleasure to always be there for you and your family, King."

"We are blessed to have you, Spindle."

Spindle blushed but changed the subject for he felt uncomfortable with all the praise, "Have you figured out if this box holds the Medallion?"

"We know it contains something but not sure what it is. It could be the Medallion. I want to be sure that it is not a danger to any of us if we open it. It could release Dark Magic. I do not want that unleashed. We already have enough of that with Elowen."

"Yes, I agree." Spindle stuttered, "Is…is Serena busy right now, King? I wanted to stop by to see her. It's been a while since we spoke more than a few words."

"Hmm, I see. Yes, just go inside and ask Solinara. She may have some pie for you to sample," Gateskin grinned as he watched Spindle fly over to his house.

"Pie? Really? I love her pies!" Spindle exclaimed as he flew to the house without another word and spoke with the Queen who was waiting there with a slice just the right size for the Sprite.

"Wow, thank you, Queen Solinara, I can't wait to try it!"

"You have earned this slice, Spindle, for all you do for us," the Queen responded.

Serena heard Spindle's voice and came out of her room to see him.

"Well, hello stranger. It's been a while since we spoke more than a few words. What's going on with you? Are you too busy to visit?"

"I just said the same thing to the King, Serena. Sorry, I, umm, was just enjoying your mother's gooseberry pie. It is delicious!"

Solinara winked at him and excused herself to give the two a little space to talk.

"What have you been doing lately?" Serena inquired with a frown.

"Well, I have been hanging around trying to protect you and your siblings, doing everything the King tells me to do, besides helping my father and mother. Father is still not at full strength but getting stronger every day. I also did some work in my uncle Micah's treehouse. He doesn't know how to build like we do. He is learning slowly."

"Thank you for all of that, Spindle," Serena stated, with a sigh. "I guess you have been busy,"

"My pleasure, Princess," he said, with a wink.

"What else is new?" Serena waited for him to say that he missed her.

"I…I…have been wanting to see you. I've missed you, Serena."

Serena's face blushed as she smiled at Spindle whose own face blushed in response turning a few shades of green.

"Well, I was hoping you would say that, Spindle. I missed you too." Serena winked at him.

"Maybe we can go on a picnic by the falls soon, Serena, when you are not busy."

"I would like that. Would you be packing the lunch or will I have to do it?" Serena giggled.

"Well, we could do it together."

"I suspected you would say that. Don't worry, Spindle, I will make the lunch and you will find the perfect spot for our picnic."

"Sounds good to me! Well, I'd better get back to help my mother. She needs me to pick some fronds and other greens for supper. See you soon, Serena. Please thank your mother for the delicious pie."

"Okay, bye, Spindle." Serena went back to her room with a dreamy look on her face.

***

Back in Parotovina the King and Queen were not as happy with each other.

Queen Beregina heard about the search for the Medallion and about some silver that was discovered in Mt. Ailylene.

"Why didn't you tell me about this search and what was found, Kaposkaran?"

"I was going to do that soon, my queen." King Kaposkaran did not meet his wife's eyes for she would know he wasn't being sincere. She could always see right through him.

"Did you also know about the silver?"

"Silver? What silver?"

"Aha, your spies did not share that with you. I wonder why?"

"I…I…must have forgotten about that. I was more interested in the Medallion. That is much more valuable. It may contain some strange powers along with Dark Magic."

"I thought you did not like Dark Magic, Kaposkaran."

"Well, yes, I don't like it when you use it. You cannot control it. If I had to use it, I would learn how to control it to benefit me."

"I understand. If it benefits you, that is all you are concerned about. Am I right?"

"Well, of course. It must be controlled and work for me. I am the King after all!"

The Queen did not retort but walked away in a huff, mumbling to herself.

King Kaposkaran sent his men to go to Sovorotskina once again to spy on the King and find out what he was doing with the box and silver that was discovered. He wanted to know everything.

The men bowed before him, listened to the King's instructions, and hurried away as Kaposkaran watched them leave, from his tower room.

What these men did not know was what they would find in Sovorotskina, for there were some who were waiting for them.

***

Spindle had heard from his fellow Sprites about the men from Parotovina. These Sprites, who bordered the village of Parotovina, were ever vigilant and warned Spindle that this could be trouble coming his way.

As Spindle headed to the King's home to report this, he spotted the two former Quintaroons out for a walk with Simon and Catalina following close behind to watch over them. Quintal and Taron were in deep discussion about what they could do if they could turn back into Quintaroons.

Spindle shook his head in disbelief, knowing that he would have to keep an eye on these two men also.

***

Unbeknownst to everyone, a spark flashed by and disappeared into the UT.

THE END for now

Stay tuned for the next book in this series.

ABOUT THE AUTHOR

Janice Spina is a retired administrative secretary from a public school system in Massachusetts. She has always loved writing poetry, novels, and children's stories. She published her first book in 2013 and has not stopped since.

This is the 46th book Janice has published. She also has two mystery series of six books each, one for boys and the other for girls even though they both are enjoyed by either sex. She has published 22 children's stories for young children. She also writes under J.E. Spina and has published eight novels and a short story collection for 18+.

She can be reached at these links.

Website: http://Jemsbooks.com
Twitter:
http://twitter.com/janice_spina

FB Main Page:
http://facebook.com/janice.spina.9
FB Author Page:
http://facebook.com/janicespina7
FB Novelist Page:
http://facebook.com/jespina7
Blog: http://Jemsbooks.wordpress.com

Janice lives in New Hampshire with her husband, John, and two tanks of fish. John is the illustrator of her children's books and designer of all her book covers.

If you enjoyed this book, please leave a review where you purchased it and spread the word to your family and friends. Janice loves to hear from readers and welcomes reviews from wherever her books are purchased. She says, 'It's like Christmas each time I receive a review!'

If you would like to be on Janice Spina's email list to receive updates, newsletters, and special deals on books, please follow her blog at link above.

Watch for more books coming from Jemsbooks.

A NOTE FROM THE AUTHOR

Book 1 of this series was written over ten years ago. At that time, I wasn't ready to publish it. There were too many other books I wanted to publish first. I've always enjoyed reading fantasy and wanted to create my own fantasy series for young adults. This is Book 3 in the continuing saga of Gateskin Chronicles.

This series is written for young adults – Ages 13-17, but can be enjoyed by adults too. I consider this series to be PG-13 and up. It is up to parents to use their discretion about whether your children read this series. Some things may not be suitable for younger children. There is never any vulgar language in any of my books but there are some situations that may be too violent for younger readers.

I hope you enjoyed this work of fiction. Watch for more books in this series coming over the next few years.

Thank you for purchasing one of Jemsbooks. I appreciate your kind support of me and my books. If you like this book, a review would be greatly appreciated wherever you purchased it. Reviews and word of mouth are the best way to spread your thoughts about books. Please share your review with friends and family. I would love to hear from you. You can reach me at jjspina@comcast.net.

All my books are available on Amazon and Barnes & Noble. Watch for more books coming for all ages.

With Blessings & Love,

Janice Spina

YA BOOKS BY JANICE SPINA - PG 13+

The Legend of the Taken Ones (Gateskin Chronicles Book 1)

The Unknown Territory (Gateskin Chronicles Book 2)

More books coming in this six-book series

OTHER MG/PT/YA BOOKS BY JANICE SPINA - 10+

Davey & Derek Junior Detectives Book 1: The Case of the Missing Cell Phone
(Pinnacle Book Achievement Award, Honorable Mention- Readers' Favorite Book Award)

Davey & Derek Junior Detectives Book 2: The Case of the Mysterious Black Cat
(Pinnacle Book Achievement Award)

Davey & Derek Junior Detectives Book 3: The Case of the Magical Ivory Elephant
(Pinnacle Book Achievement Award & Reader's Favorite Book Awards - Silver Medal)

Davey & Derek Junior Detectives Book 4: The Case of the Brown Scraggly Dog
(Finalist in Red City Review Awards & 5-Star Book Review - Readers' Favorite Book Awards)

Davey & Derek Junior Detectives Book 5:
The Case of the Sad Mischievous Ghost
Pinnacle Book Achievement Award & Authorsdb

Cover Contest - Silver Medal)

Davey & Derek Junior Detectives Book 6: The Case of the Mystery of the Bells
(Pinnacle Book Achievement Award, Finalist - Readers' Favorite Book Awards, Finalist - Book Excellence Awards)

Abby & Holly School Dance
(Pinnacle Book Achievement Award & Bronze Medal from Readers' Favorite Book Awards)

Abby & Holly Series Book 2: Unfortunate Events
Pinnacle Book Achievement Award, Readers' Favorite Book Awards - Honorable Mention)

Abby & Holly Series, Book 3, Secrets of the Trunk

(Pinnacle Book Achievement Award)

Abby & Holly Series, Book 4, The Hidden Stairway

(Pinnacle Book Achievement Award)

Abby & Holly Series, Book 5, The Copper Key

(Pinnacle Book Achievement Award)

Abby & Holly Series, Book 6, Faulty Timeline

(Pinnacle Book Achievement Award)

BOOKS BY J.E. SPINA FOR 17+

The Misunderstood Angel (Branyrd the Angel Series Book 1)

Mission of Hope (Branyrd the Angel Series Book 2)

Mission of Love (Branyrd the Angel Series Book 3)

More books coming in 2024 and beyond

BOOKS BY J.E. SPINA FOR 18+

Hunting Mariah (Finalist in Authorsdb First Lines Contest)

Mariah's Revenge (Finalist in Authorsdb First Lines Contest)

How Far is Heaven

An Angel Among Us: A Short Story Collection

In A Second

Lubelia Alycea: One Hundred Years

www.ingramcontent.com/pod-product-compliance
Lightning Source LLC
LaVergne TN
LVHW020514100826
845148LV00010B/1231